Too many deaths . . .

"Thanks, Chris," Talli said. "I did need someone to talk to."

Chris smiled and climbed out of the car. He was about to say good night when he remembered something else. He opened the door and climbed back into the Pinto.

"What is it?" Talli asked. "Something wrong?"

"There's one thing I didn't tell you," Chris said. "You remember I said that there were six deaths in the county the week before Volker came, and five the week after?"

"Yeah. What about it?"

Chris took a deep breath. "I checked every week from then till now. There was one week with nine deaths, but that was only because of a big car accident. Besides that one, no week had more than seven deaths."

"So?"

"So this week there were eleven," Chris said.

Talli stared at him in stunned silence. "You think there's another monster?" she asked after several seconds. Chris could hear the panic in her voice. "Another one like Volker?"

"You said he made others like himself," Chris said. He reached across in the darkness and found Talli's hands. "Talli, are you sure you got them all?"

Don't miss the other two books in this terrifying trilogy:

The Principal
*The Coach**

Read these thrillers from HarperPaperbacks!

Baby-sitter's Nightmare
Sweet Dreams
Sweetheart
Teen Idol
Running Scared
by Kate Daniel

And look for

Class Trip
by Bebe Faas Rice

* coming soon

THE SUBSTITUTE

M. C. Sumner

For Sarah, who put up with being a substitute and never became a monster—just the world's best teacher.

And my thanks to the Alternate Historians, as always.

HarperPaperbacks A Division of HarperCollinsPublishers
10 East 53rd Street, New York, N.Y. 10022

Produced by Daniel Weiss Associates, Inc., 33 West 17th Street, New York, New York 10011.

First printing: April 1994

Printed in the United States of America

10 9 8 7 6 5 4 3 2 1

One

Sunday

The telephone pole was covered with posters.

Winter rains had yellowed the paper and made some of the words hard to read, but Chris Delany could still make out the pictures. There was a smiling teenage face centered on every one of the fading sheets. From the fancy dresses on the girls, Chris figured that most of the pictures had been intended as senior graduation shots. Even as the car pulled away from the corner, he could still see their smiling eyes under letters that spelled out "Missing" or "Reward."

"You sure you want to move here?" he asked.

His sister, Donna, took her eyes off the rain-soaked road long enough to look over at him. "Isn't it a little early to be skeptical?" she asked.

"We're not even to Westerberg yet."

Chris looked back over his shoulder as the telephone pole with its burden of posters vanished in the mist and rain. He opened his mouth to explain his reluctance, but he stopped himself. What his sister was doing was hard enough without his making it worse. "It'll be fine," he said.

Donna nodded and turned her attention back to the road. Chris sank down into his seat and stared out across the fields along the side of the road.

Farmhouses passed at wide intervals. Between them were gray barns whose sheet-metal roofs sagged with age. Black crows sat on fence posts, hunched against the fine rain. A billboard went past, advertising a motel a few miles down the road. It was the first sign that Westerberg really existed.

It was all so different from what Chris was used to. Back in Chicago, this place had sounded kind of exotic. From close up, it all just seemed empty.

A thought sprang to Chris's mind. "Do they have a library?" he asked.

Donna glanced at him again, her dark hair swinging out as she turned her head. "What kind of town doesn't have a library?"

"Did you see it?" insisted Chris.

"I don't remember. It was probably downtown, but I wasn't really looking for it." She pushed the gearshift down a notch as the old

Dodge struggled up a steep hill. "Besides, there's a community college right outside of town," she added. "There's bound to be a library there."

Chris relaxed. Funny as things looked around this place, if there was a library, there was civilization.

He looked over at his sister and saw that she was again intent on her driving. That was the word for Donna—"intent." When their parents had died the year before, it was Donna who had pulled what was left of the family together. Aunts and uncles had been ready to swoop down on Chris, and bill collectors had been ready to take everything else. No one thought that tiny, pretty Donna—who looked barely old enough for high school—could take care of herself, much less handle her younger brother.

Chris could have told them otherwise. Donna might look like a kid, but she was one tough, determined woman. She had held together their fragile finances, finished her last year of college, and made sure that Chris stayed in school. If Donna thought that taking this job in Westerberg was the right thing to do, Chris was ready to believe it.

The Dodge reached the top of the hill, and a cluster of houses came into sight. "This is it," said Donna. "The town's just ahead."

Chris couldn't see much at first, except a few houses and the bare dark branches of some huge old oaks on the hill ahead. But a few moments later they were gliding into downtown Westerberg.

The buildings looked old. They were made of stone or brick, two or three stories tall, with long narrow windows that stared down on the street like disapproving eyes. The first-floor stores seemed huddled together against the gray world. Piles of dirty, melting snow lined the edges of the sidewalks. Off to the right a marble courthouse sat in a square of dead grass and bare-limbed winter trees.

"Well, what do you think?" Donna asked.

Before Chris could answer, the clouds suddenly broke and sunshine splashed across the landscape. The gloomy storefronts came alive with color, and the courthouse dome shone like polished silver. Every part of the town seemed to stand out in a way that the city never did.

The transformation from gloom to brightness was so complete, it took Chris a moment to catch his breath. "It's neat," he said at last. "It looks like something out of an old movie."

"That just what I thought," his sister said as she turned down a street between the rows of stores. "It looks like a good place to live. Maybe things won't be so complicated here."

Chris looked over at her and smiled. "I think I can live here, assuming they do have a library."

Donna laughed. "You're hopeless. When are you going to get tired of sitting around and reading?"

"Never, I hope," he replied.

A stoplight turned red at an intersection ahead, and Donna brought the Dodge to a stop. Chris studied the sidewalk as they waited for the light to change. As he watched, the door of a hardware store opened, and a girl came out.

She had red hair. Hair so bright it was like a flame in the sunshine. As she stepped up to the curb at the corner, she turned and looked at the Dodge. Her face was pale and a scattering of freckles crossed her nose. Her eyes were an incredible deep green.

Chris felt as if the air had gone out of his lungs. It wasn't just that the girl was pretty—more than pretty—there was something in her brief glance that carried a weight he had never felt before. "Who is that?"

"Who?" Donna asked.

Chris blushed, embarrassed that he had spoken aloud. "The girl at the corner."

Donna leaned forward and watched the girl hurry across the street. "Don't know her," she said. She arched an eyebrow at Chris. "Cute, huh? She'll be in your school."

"How do you know?"

"Because there's only one school in town," said Donna. "See, I told you you'd like it here."

Chris nodded, watching the red-haired girl pass out of sight around a corner. "Maybe I could even live here without a library," he said.

Donna laughed. "It must be love." The light changed and they drove on through the town.

At the end of the block, they passed another telephone pole decked out in posters for missing kids. Twenty feet later was another one.

Chris stared into the silent paper faces. If he looked closely, he could see a poster on almost every telephone pole. There were more posters tucked into the corners of the store windows. "What happened here?" he whispered.

"Did you say something?"

Chris pointed out the window. "All these missing-person posters," he said. "It seems like an awful lot for a town this size."

Donna's eyes flicked over to a passing pole for a moment. "The school administrator said something about that," she replied. "I think a bunch of students ran away earlier in the school year. There's a rumor that the guy who used to be the high-school principal was involved."

Chris didn't answer, but he wasn't satisfied with Donna's explanation. Runaways were usually loners. He had never heard of a bunch of kids all running away at the same time.

They drove on down the main street with faded paper eyes staring at them from all sides.

"Who is *that*?" Talli mumbled to herself. Then she got mad, because talking to herself was one of those things she was trying hard not to do.

They're strangers, said a voice in her head. *They could be dangerous. They could be more of* Them.

Talli risked another glance at the car. It was an old green Dodge with an out-of-state plate. The glare of the sun on its windshield made it hard to see at first, but Talli thought she could make out a girl with dark hair behind the wheel, and a guy with curly brown hair in the passenger seat. The guy looked over at her, and Talli quickly turned away.

A calmer voice, a voice that was getting harder and harder to hear, spoke up from deep inside her. *They look normal*, it said.

Doesn't matter what they look like, said the first voice, the frightened voice. *They can look like anyone*.

Talli swallowed hard and hurried across the street. She stepped over a heap of melting snow that lingered by the curb, then turned down the side street toward her car.

You've got to— started one of the voices in her head.

"Shut up," Talli cried aloud. "Shut up, shut up, shut up!" For over a month the voices had been growing louder and more insistent. Now Talli felt as if she were in the middle of a constant argument, and the bickering in her head grew more frequent every day.

She turned into a parking lot and walked up to her car, fishing in the pocket of her sweater for her car keys.

As she started to unlock the car door, a shape suddenly loomed up through the window. Talli jumped back. The keys slipped from her fingers and went clattering to the ground. Horrified, Talli stared at the familiar face of a girl with dark hair and laughing brown eyes.

"Lisa," Talli moaned. Her best friend's face hovered behind the dirty glass a moment longer, the lips moving without making a sound. Then it was gone.

Still trembling, Talli bent and picked up her keys. She reached toward the car as if it were a poisonous snake, but nothing happened. The key slid into the lock, and when the door opened, there was only the sun-warmed interior of the car. The Pinto was just as empty as it had been on the night Lisa had vanished from the car.

It was just your imagination, said a dry voice in her head. *It was all your imagination. Principal Volker, the murders, the monsters that could change shape. Lisa. Alex. All your imagination.*

Talli raised a trembling hand to her forehead and squeezed her eyes tightly shut. This dry, clinical voice was the one that frightened her the most. The things she'd lived through had been terrible, but the idea that they hadn't really happened—that they had all come out of her own tortured mind—scared Talli even more.

She stood for a moment with her hand on the car door, trying to steady her breathing. Her knees felt as if they might give out at any minute, letting her fall to the blacktop. Volker had come to town and killed her friends. He had been some kind of vampire, but not like the ones in the old stories and horror books Talli had loved so much. He had drained the life from Lisa, Alex, and maybe a dozen others. As unbelievable as it sounded, it was the truth.

If Talli could believe the dry voice, the one that said she had imagined everything, then maybe she would stop being haunted by the ghosts of the people who had died or disappeared. Maybe she would stop blaming herself.

"And maybe I would finish going completely crazy," she whispered to the empty air.

Talli slipped into the car and slammed the door behind her. The engine roared to life. She punched on the radio and turned the volume all the way up—she'd found that the crushing beat of the local rock station was the best way to drown out the chorus of voices inside her skull.

Talli pulled her old Pinto out of the parking lot and drove slowly through the center of town. With the sun shining, Westerberg looked like a fresh-scrubbed, picture-perfect town. Even the dark trunks of the old trees leaning out over Main Street looked less severe in the yellow light.

Someone was walking along the sidewalk. Talli's fingers tightened on the steering wheel as she fought off the impulse to slow down and see who it was. She had been staring at everyone lately—another habit she was trying to break. But just as she was starting to relax, Talli saw the unfamiliar green car again.

It was stopped at the convenience store at the bottom of Main Street hill. Talli slammed on the brakes, slowing to a crawl as she approached the green Dodge. The girl with the dark hair was standing beside the car, holding a map. The guy who ran the store was with her, pointing up the road to the left.

Pointing toward your house, said the scared voice, so loudly that even the music couldn't block it.

Talli turned down the street the man had been pointing to. She craned her neck to look back. The dark-haired girl was climbing into her car. Talli sped up, making several quick turns to reach her own street. As she pulled up to her house, she couldn't help but see the high fence and dark, empty windows of the house two doors down.

It was the house where Principal Volker had lived.

Even though he had been there for only a few short days, Talli would always think of it as his house. The bleak white walls of that house represented the center of all the terrible things that had happened back before Christmas.

Talli pulled into her driveway, and the walls of Volker's house were hidden by a shroud of trees. She parked the Pinto behind her father's pickup and killed the engine. With the radio off, she expected the voices in her head to start up again, but for once they were blessedly silent. Talli closed her eyes and savored the quiet.

The sound of a car behind her caught her attention. She turned to look over her shoulder and saw the same green car moving slowly up the street. Talli twisted around and crouched down in her seat, peeking out over the headrest as the car cruised slowly past her driveway. As soon as it was out of sight, Talli pushed her door open and climbed out.

Without thinking, Talli ran down the wet gravel of the driveway until she reached the end of the line of trees that bounded her yard. There she stopped and peered out into the street. The green Dodge was parked in front of Volker's house.

See? whined the frightened voice. *I knew it—I knew more of Them would come.*

Just because they're stopping at Volker's house doesn't mean they're monsters, said the calm voice, but Talli noticed that it didn't sound very sure of itself.

A moment later the car moved again, passing two more houses before pulling into a driveway that was flanked by For Sale signs. Talli let out a breath she didn't realize she had been holding. They were just people. They were looking for a house they hadn't been to before, and that was why they were driving so slowly. There was nothing to be afraid of.

Just because they didn't stop at Volker's house doesn't mean they're not *monsters*, said the frightened voice.

Talli bit her lip and marched up the gravel drive toward her house, refusing to acknowledge what the voice had said.

Her father was waiting inside the door when she came in. He gave her a curious smile. "No movies?" he asked.

"What?" Talli asked.

"Movies. Didn't you go to the video store to rent something?"

"Oh, yeah." Talli brushed her red hair back from her face and tried to smile. "I just didn't find anything I liked."

"That doesn't sound like the Tallibeth McAlister I know," her father said. "Aren't you the girl who loves every horror movie ever made?"

Talli shrugged and stepped past him. "I guess I'm tired of them," she said, hoping she sounded more normal than she felt.

"Well," Mr. McAlister called as Talli headed for the stairs. "Your mother's going to be late getting home, so you're stuck with my cooking. That should be enough horror for anyone."

Talli glanced back at him from the foot of the stairs and saw that he was looking at her with an expression of concern. He quickly covered it with a smile, but Talli had seen that expression a lot lately. It was how everyone seemed to be looking at her these days—as if she were sick. Or crazy.

Aren't we crazy? asked a voice in her skull.

Talli hurried up the stairs to her room and

shut the door. As usual, the first thing she did was turn on the radio, anxious to avoid another argument inside her head. Then she pulled off her jacket and threw it onto the bed.

"If I had someone to talk to," she whispered to the walls, "then maybe I wouldn't have all this chattering inside my skull."

But there wasn't anyone left to talk to. She couldn't go to her parents. They had stood aside while the vampire came into their house to kill Talli. And even when the tables were turned and Principal Volker went up in blue-white flames in the middle of their living-room floor, Talli's parents had acted as if nothing at all was happening. They'd slept right through it, along with the rest of the town. As far as they were concerned, nothing unusual had occurred.

If Lisa were there, Talli could have talked to her. But Lisa had vanished from Talli's car while Talli was miles away, trying to ferret out Volker's secrets.

If only Alex were here . . .

The thought of Alex made Talli's throat go tight. She sat down on the edge of her bed and fingered the old blanket. It had never occurred to her that a time would come when she wouldn't have Alex.

His picture still looked back at her from across the room. In it he was wearing a really ugly blue tuxedo, but the smile on his face was so bright that the clothes were easy to forget. Talli was beside him in the picture, looking tiny next to six-foot-tall Alex. Behind them were banners that identified the shot as the junior prom.

Talli and Alex had been together for what seemed like forever. And while they had their share of arguments—maybe more than their share—they always got back together. Alex had been smart and funny, and Talli had loved him more than she'd realized. She had been so used to his being there that he had become something she took for granted—like air, like water.

Now Alex was dead.

Volker had trapped Alex and Talli in a room before they knew what he really was. Talli had been able to shake off Volker's power and escape. But Alex hadn't. Talli had left him frozen in a chair, hypnotized and helpless. And she had never seen him again.

Talli got up from the bed and walked across the room. She ran a finger across the smooth glass that covered the picture of Alex's smile. Closing her eyes, she took a deep breath and pushed Alex's picture facedown on the dresser.

If only you hadn't left him alone, said one of the voices. *If you hadn't abandoned him, Alex wouldn't be dead.*

Two

Alex opened his eyes.

He was hungry. That wasn't surprising. It seemed that he was always hungry—driven by an ache that could never be satisfied. Few other thoughts ever made it past the barrier of that all-consuming need.

He pushed away the pile of loose boards and heavy cloth that covered him and looked around at a room filled with tools and paint cans. The room was dark, but Alex had no trouble seeing. Everything in the small room stood out sharply in shades of red that ranged from purple-black to a dull crimson.

Through the fog that always seemed to fill his mind, Alex tried to remember where he was. He had been in a town called Simpson the day before, he could remember that much. Before that . . . before that, he couldn't remember. For Alex the past had disappeared in a gloom of confusion. And the future promised to be as vague.

He pushed himself to his feet and shuffled across the room, overturning a paint can as he went.

There was no point in thinking about what to do next, because the answer was always the same: it was time to feed.

His hand found the doorknob and he pulled. The door was locked. Alex couldn't remember if he had locked it himself—it might have been locked by someone who had come along during the day while he was resting. It didn't matter. Alex pulled a bit harder, and the lock tore through the wooden frame around the door, bringing with it a shower of splintered wood. Alex staggered out into the fiery red night.

From outside he could see that the building he'd been sleeping in was some kind of wooden shed. Nearby was a house. Even through the walls, Alex could see that there were people inside—their forms looked like torches moving behind glass. Just seeing them made Alex's hunger flare.

Hinges creaked as the door to the house opened. One of the bright figures stepped out onto the front steps. In the light from the open door, Alex could see that it was an older man with a fringe of snow-white hair on a mostly bald head. There was a narrow object in his hand. Some part of Alex's mind realized that it was a gun.

"Who's out here?" called the man on the steps.

"Steven," said a woman's voice from inside the house. "Get back inside."

"Hold on a minute," said the man. "I heard something out here." He walked slowly down the steps, moving out of the light. Alex could see him blinking his eyes, fighting to see in the darkness.

Alex walked slowly forward until he was standing no more than an arm's length from the old man.

The man sensed something and raised his gun. "Who's there?" he whispered.

"No one," said Alex. The gun barrel swung toward him, but Alex stepped to the side. Too late, the old man seemed to realize how far he had gone into the darkness. He glanced over his shoulder at the pool of light around the front of the house. He started to take a step back.

Alex's hands flashed out of the darkness. One palm went over the man's mouth, the other arm circled his throat. The gun fell to the ground as Alex pulled him away from the light, heading through the woods and down to the edge of the water. The man's heels thrashed helplessly against the fallen pine needles. Alex leaned his face close to the old man's.

"Don't fight," he said.

The man's eyes were wide, and his skin had gone cold under Alex's palm. Alex wanted to say something more, to try to calm the man, but the hunger rose up like a storm. He reached out, sending a dark stream of . . . something into the man. Without even understanding how he was doing it, Alex pulled.

Ropes of red fire spilled out of the man, and Alex sighed. For a moment the hunger was satisfied. But all too quickly the flames inside the man were down to a flicker. The hunger pushed at Alex, demanding that last little bit of energy, but Alex dropped the man, letting him fall into the reeds at the edge of the water. The old man hit the ground with a thump and lay still. If Alex hadn't been able to see the faint plume of warmth that still rose from the man's mouth, he would have thought the man was dead.

"Steven!" called the woman from the house. "Steven! Get back up here where I can see you."

Alex stepped through the dark trees, back toward the woman. There was no panic in her voice yet, only irritation. Alex stopped at the edge of the darkness and waited.

"Steven? What are you doing?" She moved out onto the steps and let the door swing shut behind her. "Steven?" There was a hint of fear in her voice now. Alex could smell it like the odors that came from a kitchen at dinnertime.

The old man had taken the edge off his hunger, and Alex was able to wait patiently while the woman slowly descended the steps, stopping to call to the old man every few seconds. She was much younger than the man had been. Alex wondered for a second if she was the man's wife, but he didn't think about it long. Who she was wasn't important. What was important was that the fire inside her was much brighter.

It took several long minutes for her to work up the courage to step out into the blackness. Alex took her under the dark trees, his face pressed into her hair as he fed. When there was nothing left in her but a tiny glow, he pulled himself away.

His head spun. He had never before fed twice in such a short time. He ran his hand along the soft fabric of the woman's dress and smiled in the dark. Carefully, he lowered her to the mossy ground and left her sitting against the rough bark of an oak tree. Feeling invigorated as never before, Alex walked around the house and up the long drive toward the road beyond.

It took him several hours to get a ride. Traffic was sparse along the narrow highway, and three cars passed before a red station wagon pulled over in response to Alex's wagging thumb. Alex ran up to the car and hopped into the passenger seat.

"Thanks," he said.

"No problem," said the driver. He looked to be in his late twenties, with a very short haircut and a pair of heavy glasses. "Where are you heading?" he asked.

"Atlanta," said Alex. He actually had no idea where he was going, or even what direction the car was headed. Atlanta was simply the first thing that popped into his mind.

The man laughed. "You're a long, long way from there. Look, I'll take you as far as Stroud City. I'm going on to Westerberg, myself, but the state highway doesn't run through there. You'd probably have better luck getting a ride south if you stay on the main roads."

Alex didn't reply for a moment. Westerberg. There was something about that name that sounded familiar. Had he hunted there before he had gone to Simpson? It seemed more important than that, somehow. "Sounds good," he said at last.

He leaned back against the door frame and wondered whether he should take the man now, or wait until they reached Stroud City.

Three

Monday

The alarm clock wailed like a banshee. Chris stuck one hand out from under the blankets and batted at the clock, but he missed. He tried again, with no more luck. Finally, he had to roll over and open one eye before finding the clock and slapping the button that killed the alarm.

For a moment he couldn't remember where he was. This bleak room with sterile white walls sure didn't look like his poster-covered bedroom. Instead of being on the bedside table, the alarm clock was lying on a bare wood floor. Chris sat up, trying to recall why he wasn't at home. Then he remembered that this was home. The house back in Chicago was gone, sold. This place was home now.

Sunlight was leaking in around a sheet he had tacked up over the window. Donna hadn't gotten around to buying curtains. Aside from the mattress on the floor, the only furniture in Chris's room was the suitcase that contained his clothes.

There was a knock at the door. "Chris? You up?"

He slumped back down on the mattress and pulled the pillow over his head. "No," he said.

The door squeaked as Donna pushed it open and stepped into the room. "You better get up soon," she said. "I've got to take off in about ten minutes."

Chris peeked out from under the pillow. "Do we really have to go to school today?" he asked. "I mean, we just got into town and everything."

Donna grabbed the pillow away from him. "Come on," she said. "I'm the teacher. They kind of expect me to be there every day." She thumped him over the head with the pillow. "You better get up, or you'll be late."

Chris rubbed his eyes and squinted at the clock. It read six thirty. Chris groaned. "This is too early, even for a school day."

"I have to go early to get my room set up, and I'm supposed to be there at least half an hour before school starts." Donna tossed the pillow back onto Chris's bed and stood up straight. "How do I look?" she asked.

Chris glanced at her quickly. "Great," he said. "You look great." That was easy enough to say, because Donna would have looked great even if she had been wearing dirty coveralls. Ever since grade school, Chris had been fielding requests from guys who wanted to meet his sister.

"What I mean is, do I look like a teacher?"

Chris looked at her more closely. The tailored suit she was wearing certainly looked like something an older teacher might wear. On Donna it only emphasized how slender she was, and made her look like a teenager wearing her mother's clothes. Chris knew better than to say that. "It doesn't look quite like you," he said.

"But does it look like a teacher?"

"Yeah, I guess it looks like a teacher."

Donna smiled nervously. "Thanks." She glanced over at the clock. "You better get moving if you want to ride with me." She walked quickly out of Chris's room. He could hear the heels of her "sensible teacher shoes" clacking against the wood floor.

Chris sat up and ran his fingers through his sleep-tangled hair. "Do I have a choice?" he called after her.

"You could always walk. It's about a mile and a half, and it's a pretty straight shot." Donna came back down the hall and leaned into the bedroom. "You want directions?"

Chris thought for a moment, then shook his head. "Give me a minute. I'll go with you."

"One minute is about what you've got," said

Donna. "I'm going to grab something to eat. See you at the door." She hurried away.

Chris pushed back the sheets of his makeshift bed and looked around. It would be a another day before the moving van showed up with the rest of their things. In the meantime they had to get by on what they had hauled with them in the car.

He climbed up off the mattress and shuffled over to the suitcase. He started to pull out a pair of jeans and stopped. The contents of the suitcase were pretty messy. It sure didn't look like the neat way that his mother used to pack. For a moment Chris felt the familiar pain in his heart. Even after almost a year, the thought that his parents were gone could still take him by surprise.

If I only knew who did it, he thought. Right after they died, the Chicago police had come and interviewed Chris, Donna, and everyone in their neighborhood. It seemed as if they were working hard at solving the murder. Chris had tried to learn all he could about the investigation, but the police weren't exactly thrilled to have a high-school student asking them questions all the time. Days had turned into weeks, and still the police didn't have a suspect. A few more weeks, and the answer they gave to Chris was always the same: "No progress."

After a couple of months Chris realized the police were never going to have a suspect. They had given up. Intellectually, he knew why they had stopped their investigation. Hundreds of people died in the city every year. The police couldn't spend too much time investigating any one murder. If a case didn't show some progress, they had little choice but to give up and move on to the next one.

Chris understood it perfectly . . . in his mind. But down in his guts, he knew he would never forgive the police for not finding his parents' killers.

This kind of thinking never helps anything, Chris thought. Clearing his mind, he took a deep breath and pulled on his jeans. He grabbed a sweatshirt out of the heap in the suitcase and walked over to the window while he tugged it over his head. He yanked back one corner of the sheet that covered the window and looked out.

The gloomy weather had vanished with the night. The sun was peeking over the horizon, lighting a sky that was pale winter blue and completely free of clouds. From Chris's room on the second floor, he could see blocks of winter-brown grass and bare trees. The whole town looked much cheerier than it had the day before. The yards were wider than he was used to—each house sat back from the street in a square of grass and trees.

Donna knocked at the door again and stuck her head into the room without waiting for Chris to reply. "Ready to go?" she asked.

Chris dropped the sheet back over the window. "Maybe I will walk," he said. "That way I'll at least have time for breakfast."

"Okay. To get there, you walk down this road, then turn right through downtown. The school's at the bottom of the hill." Donna smiled nervously. "Wish me luck."

Chris smiled back. "Don't worry. You'll do great, as usual."

Donna turned and hurried down the steps. Thirty seconds later she hurried back up them. "Um, I don't suppose you know where I put the car keys?" she asked sheepishly.

Chris couldn't help laughing. "You left them on the kitchen table. I saw them last night."

"Right," she said. "Kitchen table." She charged out of the room again, and a minute later Chris heard her slam the door. Moments after that the car's engine rumbled to life as Donna headed for school. He looked out the window in time to see the old Dodge sweep along the street and vanish behind the trees.

Chris finished dressing and headed downstairs for some breakfast. The house still felt empty—all of the rooms he passed were bare of furniture and the windows were uncovered. The few things that they had been able to load into Donna's car barely made a dent in the big old house. Chris hated the lonely feeling it gave him. He couldn't wait for the moving truck to show up. After breakfast Chris ran back upstairs and grabbed a jacket and his current book. It was an Agatha Christie mystery. Chris had been through all her books at least three times, but he hadn't gotten tired of them yet. He did a quick count of the remaining pages, making sure that he had enough to last until he got home. There was nothing worse than running out of things to read in the middle of a lunch hour or study hall.

His crumpled backpack was stowed in the suitcase. When he opened it to put in his book, he found it still loaded with the notebooks and supplies he had used at his old school. It was strange how the things he had been using only a couple of weeks before already looked like something from another lifetime.

He went downstairs, locked the door carefully, and stepped out onto the porch. The day had looked bright from inside, but the air was still crisp. Chris slung his backpack over his shoulder and pulled the front of his jacket closed. Hunching his shoulders against the chilly breeze, he started up the street.

The house two doors down from theirs caught his attention as he passed. It was bigger than the others in the neighborhood, with tall white sides that rose up above the trees. A board fence blocked the view of the first floor, making the house look mysterious. Judging by the curtainless windows and weeds along the edge of the drive, Chris figured that the house was empty. He walked on, thinking idly that the old place would make a great haunted house at Halloween.

He had gone only another half block when an orange car suddenly backed out of a driveway in front of him. The driver turned toward him as she shifted out of reverse, and Chris caught a glimpse of red hair and bright green eyes before she turned back and sped away.

"Wow," Chris said under his breath.

"She's nuts," said a voice at Chris's back.

Chris spun around and found another guy standing close behind him. "Who are you?" he asked.

The guy was almost painfully thin. He wore a faded denim jacket that was long enough for the sleeves to come down over his hands, and a red baseball cap shoved so far down his forehead that Chris could barely see his eyes. "You must be the new guy," he said. "The one that took the Deveraux house."

Chris shrugged. "I guess. Who are you?" he repeated.

"I'm Paul Katz." The guy lifted an arm and a pale hand emerged from the jacket. He raised a pair of fingers to his forehead and gave Chris a casual salute.

"Chris Delany," Chris replied.

Katz nodded. "Where you from?"

"Chicago." Chris jerked his head in the direction that the orange car had gone. "Why did you say that girl is crazy?"

"Because she is." Katz shoved his hidden hands into the pockets of his jeans and started walking. Chris looked at him for a moment and then fell in beside him.

"She's been nuts since everybody disappeared," Katz continued. "Guess I can't blame her, what with her boyfriend being gone, and all."

"She's got a boyfriend?" Chris asked.

The other boy snorted and looked at him from under the bill of his cap. "Not anymore she doesn't. I figure he's as dead as the rest of them."

"The rest of them?" Chris was having a hard time keeping up with the conversation.

Katz stopped suddenly. "I'm going in here," he said, pointing at a pale-green house. "Getting a ride with my cousin."

"Oh."

"You want a ride?"

Chris shook his head. "I thought I'd walk this morning—get to see what the town looks like."

The skinny boy gave him another nod. "Be careful, Chris Delany. This place may look safe, but don't be fooled," he said. Then he turned and walked quickly up the steps to the green house.

Chris watched him go inside before starting down the street again. What Katz said didn't fit well with what Donna had told Chris about the posters. Katz didn't make it sound as if the students had run away. He made it sound as if they were dead. In fact, he made the whole town sound like a death trap.

Trying to scare the new guy, Chris thought. He walked on down the street, looking at the well-tended houses and their well-tended yards. Westerberg certainly didn't look like a place where a lot of people might have been killed. But considering the size of the town, Chris could easily believe it was the kind of place a lot of kids might run away from.

A couple of blocks later, he left the residential area and entered the small downtown business district. Since it was still early in the morning, most of the windows were dark and most of the parking spots were empty. Several of the stores looked as if they had recently gone out of business, and their vacant windows still held fading decorations that dated back to Christmas or Thanksgiving. Chris couldn't shake the feeling that there was something ominous about this place—with all these abandoned shops, Main Street looked like a ghost town.

As he reached the middle of the town, Chris was excited to spot a dark metal sign that announced the Calloway County Library. It was a narrow brick building wedged between two taller stores. Chris pressed his face close to the glass door and looked inside. Rows of dark shelves filled the space. It might not be as big as the libraries back in Chicago, but it looked as if it was packed with books.

Chris turned away from the window with a smile. With any luck at all, he should be able to find a good stock of mysteries in there. He continued down the street with his mood considerably brighter. The things that Paul Katz had said seemed very remote, and even the town didn't bother him as much.

At the corner was the one traffic light that divided downtown Westerberg. It was red, and Chris dutifully waited for the lights to go through their cycle, even though there wasn't a car in sight. As he waited, he noticed one of the posters on the telephone pole next to him.

Chris walked over to the pole and squinted at the poster. Rain and sun had turned the picture on the paper a pale sepia, but he could still make out the smile of a very pretty girl with a mane of blond hair. In the fine print at the bottom of the poster were the vital statistics:

> Samantha Deveraux
> Height: 5' 6"
> Weight: 112
> Hair: Blond   Eyes: Blue
> Missing since November 16.

Samantha Deveraux. Chris looked at the faded photo and back at the name. Hadn't Paul Katz asked if he had moved into the Deveraux house? With a strange chill Chris realized he was probably living in the house where Samantha Deveraux had lived before she disappeared.

He wondered how he could find out for sure.

Talli sat up in bed. It was cool in her room, but sweat glued her nightshirt to her body. Chill beads of it trickled down her face. She swallowed hard, refusing to let the scream that had gathered at the back of her throat escape. The last thing she wanted to do was give her parents another reason to worry about her.

The nightmares had been coming off and on since all the deaths back in November. For the past few weeks they had been getting easier, but this had been one of the most violent ones ever. And the worst part of every nightmare was waking up and remembering that what had really happened was even worse than the dreams.

The sky outside her window was starting to lighten with dawn. Talli got out of bed and stripped off her damp nightshirt. The brisk air felt good against her skin. She closed her eyes for a moment and just stood there in the dark, letting the dream die in her mind and enjoying the silence.

Then she opened the drawers of her dresser slowly, trying not to make any noise, and fished for clothes in the dark. As she got dressed, the sun gradually heaved itself over the horizon, lighting the tops of the surrounding trees, and gleaming from the upper floors of nearby houses. Talli glanced toward the window and saw the light glinting against the bare windows of Volker's empty house.

We should go over there, said one of the voices in her head. *Maybe Alex and Lisa are still hidden there somewhere. Maybe we could find them.*

Talli shivered and turned away from the window. There was no way she was ever going back into that house. No way. The things that had happened there were the things that filled her nightmares. After a moment she pulled the shades closed.

It was still an hour early when Talli headed downstairs for breakfast. Her father, wearing his police uniform, was perched at the kitchen table, holding a cup of coffee in one hand and the flimsy local paper in the other. He snorted softly at something as he read.

Talli's mother came out of the kitchen with a plate of bacon in her hand. "Good morning," she said to Talli with a smile. "Sleep well?"

Talli noticed that her mother spoke very carefully. These days her parents were always careful about what they said, as if they thought Talli might break. Ever since Alex, Lisa, and all the others had "disappeared," they seemed to expect Talli to vanish at any moment as well.

Mr. McAlister looked up from his paper and

gave Talli a cautious smile. "Hi, Tal," he said. "Ready to start back to school?"

Talli nodded and sat down at the table. She wasn't hungry, but she took a strip of bacon from the plate just to make her mother feel better.

"I think it'll be a good thing for you to get back in classes," Mrs. McAlister said. "With the time you took off after all the trouble, and then the long Christmas break, it'll be nice to get back to a regular schedule."

"Absolutely," Mr. McAlister added. "It'll be good for you to get out of the house and back into things."

Talli stared down at the table, afraid to look at their faces. "Sure," she said. "It'll be . . ." She trailed off, unable to find the right word.

There were a few seconds of uncomfortable silence before her mother spoke again. "I'm sure everyone in the drama club will be happy to see you."

A series of images flashed through Talli's mind: a grinning guy holding a knife on her in the prop room . . . the tall form of Principal Volker standing in the shadows behind the stage. And worst of all, the memory of running through the inky darkness of the empty auditorium, falling and crying, as some nameless horror came clawing after her in the blackness.

"Tal," said her father. His big hand closed on her shoulder, and his fingers squeezed gently. "Tallibeth? You all right?"

Talli nodded quickly. "I'm fine." She tried to smile, but her face felt numb. "I'll be glad to get back into things," she mumbled.

Mrs. McAlister glanced over at her husband, then sat down in the chair on Talli's right. "Talli, honey, we've had another talk with the school counselor," she said.

Talli sighed. "Why did you do that?"

"We're worried about you," said Mr. McAlister. He took his hand off her shoulder. "We know how tough it was to have so many of your friends leave town."

They didn't leave town, Talli thought furiously, but she said nothing.

"We think you're having a hard time bouncing back," continued her mother. "We don't want you doing anything rash. That's why we talked to Dr. Anthony again."

"And what did he have to say?" Talli asked.

Mrs. McAlister pulled a white card from the pocket of her slacks and laid it on the kitchen table. "He told us about someone that he thought could help you," she said. "I—" She stopped and looked over at Talli's father. "I mean we. We've already made an appointment for you."

Talli picked up the card and turned it over. "Dr. Aston, psychiatry," she read aloud. There was an address and phone number under the name, and at the bottom of the card was a line of smaller text in italics. "Specializing in the problems of adolescents," she said.

Mrs. McAlister touched Talli lightly on the arm. "Please tell us you'll go," she said softly.

Talli started to protest, but stopped herself. Weren't psychiatrists supposed to be able to keep things to themselves? Wasn't there a law that kept them from telling what their patients said? Maybe she could talk to this Dr. Aston If she could talk to someone, maybe it *would* make a difference.

"I'll go," Talli said. "When's the appointment?"

Her mother leaned back in her chair. For the first time that morning, her smile seemed genuine. "It's next weekend," she said.

Mr. McAlister leaned close to Talli and spoke in a mock whisper. "I'm glad you decided to go," he said. "It'll make your mother feel better."

Talli hurried through the rest of breakfast and went back upstairs to get ready for school. Now that she had agreed to it, the idea of going to a psychiatrist didn't sound so bad. She almost felt like whistling as she shoved her things into an oversize purse.

What do you think this Dr. Aston will do if you start talking about monsters? asked a voice in her head. *Talking about people that can change their shape and girls that age from eighteen to eighty in a week?*

"He can't say anything," Talli whispered to herself. "Doctors can't tell what they hear from their patients. It's the law."

He doesn't have to tell what you said to tell everyone that you're crazy.

"So I'll say that it was kidnappers or serial killers," Talli whispered angrily. "I don't have to tell the truth about everything I saw."

Talli tried her best to ignore the voices as she hurried downstairs and out to her car. As she approached the orange Pinto, she expected to see Lisa waiting for her, but the window was empty. Talli hopped into the driver's seat, cranked the engine, and backed down the driveway. The car bounced out onto the road, and Talli was about to drive on when she caught a glimpse of someone standing outside the car.

There was a guy on the sidewalk. She looked at him in surprise, and he looked back with an expression that mirrored her own shock. His face seemed familiar, but it took Talli a moment to remember where she had seen him before. The green Dodge. He had been the guy in the green car.

The voices broke out anew. *He is one of Them—he's following you.*

Talli put the car into gear and drove off, leaving the guy standing by the curb. "He's just a guy who moved in down the street," she said as she turned on the radio. "He looks nice. He's not a monster."

But there are monsters, the voices chorused. *Real monsters.*

Four

Alex glanced over at the man behind the wheel. They were still thirty miles away from Stroud City, and already the sky in the east was growing red as dawn approached.

Even though he had fed twice already, the hunger had been gnawing at Alex for hours. As always, the more the hunger called, the less room there was for thinking.

"Can you drive faster?" he asked.

The man smiled. "You in some kind of a hurry?"

Alex fixed his eyes on the man and said nothing. He couldn't remember how to speak—couldn't think of anything except the glow of life pouring from the man. It pulled at Alex. Something deep inside him screamed out with the desire to feed.

The man looked over at Alex with concern. "You feeling all right, kid? You don't look so good."

"I'm fine," Alex said. It took all his will to turn away from the man and look out at the countryside. The clouds on the horizon were stained a bloody red by the rising sun. While the daylight no longer caused Alex the agony it once had, every moment spent in it would weaken him. And increase his hunger.

Alex turned on the driver. The man's eyes bulged in their sockets as Alex's hand closed around his throat. He took his hands from the steering wheel and clawed at Alex's arm.

Alex pulled the living energy from him as swiftly as an animal snatches up its food. The power slid into him like a river of light, making everything seem brighter. He smiled in the darkness as he removed his hand and let the man slump against the door. Through it all, he gave no thought to the fact that the car was speeding down the highway at over sixty miles an hour.

He looked up just as the car plowed through a flimsy metal guardrail at the side of the road. Alex tried to grab the wheel, but it was far too late to save the car from disaster. It glanced off a dozen small pine trees, tore through a patch of brush, bounced into the air, and began to tumble nose over tail down a steep rocky slope.

Alex tumbled about the interior of the car, banging into his unconscious victim. The windshield smashed against a rock, and the air was suddenly full of broken glass. On the third bounce, the passenger-side door flew open. Another half turn, and Alex was flung from the car.

For a second he seemed to hover high in the predawn air. Below him the car continued in its destructive path down the hill. Then gravity remembered Alex, and he fell to the stony hillside.

His left leg hit the ground first. The sound of his bones breaking was as clear and loud as a string of pistol shots. Then it was his chest against the rocks. Alex could feel his ribs breaking, feel the jagged shards of bone spearing through his chest. His head hit the ground, and the night vanished in a flash of pain.

Alex opened his eyes and rolled onto his side. He knew he had been unconscious, but it must have been for mere seconds, because he could still hear rocks sliding down the slope from the passage of the car. But he could no longer feel the pain of broken ribs. He tried out his left leg and found that it moved easily.

He got to his feet and looked down the hill to where the crumpled car rested on its roof. He felt tired, terribly tired, and the hunger was back stronger than ever.

Alex started climbing toward the top of the hill, but he had gone only a few feet before the sun peeked over the horizon and lit the sky with orange light.

It hurt. It burned more painfully than it had in weeks. As it touched Alex's hands and face, his skin blackened, and smoke curled up into the morning air.

Screaming, Alex turned and half ran, half slid back down the hill. He reached the smashed car and climbed inside, huddling behind the torn seat to hide from the light. He wondered if the crash had somehow drained him, leaving him with no energy left to withstand the force of the sun.

The man who had given him a ride was slung across the front seat, still held in place by the seat belt. Alex reached out to him, trying to pull the last spark of force from the man. But there was no life left to take. The man was dead.

The sun shone down brightly. Alex whimpered and pulled himself farther down into the wreck.

Five

The school wasn't what Chris had expected. It looked appropriate on the outside, with a row of tall elm trees sheltering the walkway to the entrance—exactly what a small-town high school should be. But inside it was louder and more crowded than any school Chris had ever been stuck with in Chicago.

He had to ask directions twice before he made it to his first-period classroom. When he finally forced his way through the crowd in the room, he found all the chairs full. With a sigh Chris joined a half-dozen students standing at the back of the room.

The teacher, an older man with thinning gray hair, came into the room with a stack of folders in his hand. He dropped behind his desk and looked out at the crowded classroom with evident despair.

"We'll try to get some more desks in here by tomorrow," he said. "But I'm not promising anything." He plopped the folders down on the desk and began to call the roll.

Chris ended up sitting on the floor for the rest of the class. When the bell rang, the teacher tried to say something, but it was drowned out by the stampede of students heading for the door. Chris gathered up his things and took his place in the flood.

The rest of the classes weren't much different from the first. In two other rooms there were students who ended up without desks, though Chris was lucky enough to catch a chair in one of them. Every class seemed to be more crowded than it should be, and every teacher seemed frustrated.

By the time lunch rolled around, Chris was missing his old school more than ever. He fought his way through the packed cafeteria and took a tray.

A tall, slim girl with curly brown hair slid into line behind him and took a tray of her own. "You new here?" she asked.

"How can you tell?" asked Chris.

The girl shrugged. "You look like you're in the wrong place." She held her tray in one hand and stuck out the other. "I'm Casey Pays."

Chris gave her hand a shake and smiled at her. "Chris Delany," he said.

"Delany?" Casey cocked her head to one side

and looked at him with cool blue eyes. "Are you related to the new teacher?"

"She's my sister."

"Thought so. You kind of look like her." Casey's face broke into a broad grin. "She's great."

"I always thought so," said Chris. He slid his tray onto the counter just in time for a worker on the other side to slap down a plate of some unidentifiable gray food. Chris looked at it in disgust. "What is this stuff?"

"Turkey and dressing. At least I think so. They have better food at your last school?" Casey asked as she put her own tray on the counter.

"Nope," said Chris. "I guess cafeteria food is the same all over."

Casey laughed. "You really do remind me of your sister," she said. "I think she's going to make a great teacher."

"Donna's good at everything. She always has been." Chris paid for his lunch at the end of the line and waited for Casey to join him.

"I've got family at the school, too," she said. "My dad is the head football coach, and he helps out with baseball, too. Do you play?"

"Baseball," he said. "Maybe I'll go out for the team."

Casey nodded at the open doors on the far side of the room. "Let's go outside," she said. "It's not too cold today, and it's too crowded in here to sit down."

Chris nodded and followed her through the

press of people. They were almost to the doors when a familiar red-haired girl passed right in front of him. Chris turned around so fast that the plate of food went sliding across his tray and almost fell to the floor.

Casey stopped and looked at him over her shoulder. "You okay?"

"Yeah, fine," said Chris. He tried to point with his chin. "Who is that?"

Casey followed his gaze across the sea of people. "The redhead? That's Talli McAlister. Why? You know her from somewhere?"

Chris shook his head. "Not really. I saw her on the street yesterday." He watched as Talli went across the room and vanished through an open door.

Casey nudged him in the back with her tray. "Come on outside and talk. I'll tell you everything you want to know about Talli." She led the way through the open door to the school yard, picked out a spot on the concrete steps that came down from the door, and sat down.

Chris sat at her side on the cold steps. There were other students lunching on the long sidewalk under the elms, or camped out on the brown grass. "I'm surprised to see all these people out here in the cold," he said.

"Better than the noise inside," Casey said with a shrug. She picked up a fork and dug into the suspicious-looking turkey. "So what made you come to Westerberg?"

Now it was Chris's turn to shrug. "I came because my sister came."

"You live with her?"

"Yeah. My parents died last year. I'm staying with Donna until I get out of high school. Then I'm on my own." He frowned at the things on his plate and pushed them around with his fork. Finally he scooped up a bite. It tasted about as bad as it looked.

"That's tough," said Casey. "I mean, about your parents. Was it a car accident?"

"No. Somebody shot them. The police never figured out who."

"Oh." For a moment Casey seemed speechless, but it didn't last long. "Where'd you live before this?" she asked.

"Chicago." Chris started to lift another bite of the food to his mouth, but changed his mind and dropped it back to his plate. "What made you talk to me?" he asked suddenly. "Nobody's talked to me all day."

Casey grinned. "Sheer boredom," she said. "I've been in Westerberg all my life. Visitors from the real world are always interesting."

"Westerberg's not the real world?"

"Far from it!" Casey dropped her fork to her plate. "How long have you been here?"

"About a day," said Chris.

"Okay, one day. So tell me, how many weird things have you seen?"

Chris thought for a moment. "Well, it's

weird that the school is so crowded."

"Uh-huh," Casey prompted. "What else?"

"And there are all those people that disappeared."

"And?"

"And this morning a guy came up to me and told me that girl, Talli, was crazy."

"Is that all?" asked Casey.

Chris nodded. "I think so."

She leaned close to him and spoke in a whisper. "Don't forget the weird girl who asked you to eat lunch outside in the winter," she said. Then she laughed and leaned away. "Who was the guy?"

"What guy?" Chris asked.

"The guy that said Talli was crazy," Casey said.

"Oh," he said. "I think he said his name was Cat. Paul Cat?"

"Katz," Casey corrected him. "Katz the Rat, everyone calls him. He can never resist running his mouth off."

"Was he right? Is Talli crazy?" Chris asked.

Casey's grin widened until dimples appeared at the corners of her mouth. "You like her, don't you?"

"I don't even know her," said Chris, but he could feel a blush creeping into his cheeks.

"Yeah, but you like her," said Casey. She lifted her fork and shoveled up another bite of turkey. "Talli's nice," she said, "but she's kind of messed up right now. Her boyfriend was one of the ones that ran off last semester. Her best friend left, too. A lot of people think they might have gone together."

"I guess that would be enough to screw anyone up," Chris said with a glance back toward the lunchroom door. "Katz said that the people who were missing were really dead."

Casey snorted. "The Rat would say something like that." She scooped up the last of her turkey and started in on her applesauce. "The truth is," she said, "that no one knows where they went."

Chris thought back to all the missing-person posters that he had seen. "How many people disappeared?" he asked.

"There were about a dozen kids," Casey said. "And a few principals." She leaned forward again, punctuating her words with gestures of her fork. "You ask me, that's the really weird part."

"A *few* principals?"

She nodded. "First it was Principal Shay, then it was his replacement, a guy named Volker. And when Volker disappeared, his assistant principal did, too."

"Wow," Chris said. He thought about the mystery novel tucked safely in his locker. That plot wasn't nearly as strange as what was going on right in this little town. When his parents were murdered, Chris had felt helpless. Chicago was a large city, and two people could be killed without the police really caring much. But Westerberg was small. How could so many people vanish from a town this size without leaving a trail?

"So," Casey was saying, "you have a car?"

It took Chris a moment to wake up from his thoughts and answer her question. "No. No car. I walked here."

"You want a lift home?" she asked.

Chris looked up in surprise. "Sure, I'll take a ride." As he was speaking, he saw Talli McAlister come out the door and stand at the top of the stairs. In the sunlight her hair blazed like copper. There was a sad, distant look in her green eyes.

Casey turned her head to follow his gaze. "You'll take a ride," she said, "but you're really interested in Talli, right?"

"I—"

"Don't worry," Casey said. "I'm not going to put a move on you—you're not my type. In fact, I know Talli pretty well. I'll introduce you, if you want."

Chris pulled his eyes away from the red-haired girl and looked back at Casey. "Yeah," he said. "I do want to meet her."

"Okay, then. I'll make introductions later." She reached over with her fork and tapped it against his tray. "You going to eat that turkey?"

"Guess not," Chris said. He passed his plate

to Casey, and she immediately started in on seconds. "For someone so thin," he said, "you sure know how to eat."

Casey looked up from her plate and grinned again.

So far the day hadn't been as bad as Talli had expected. It was strange coming back to school after being out for so long. A lot of people seemed too nervous even to talk to her, and those who did say anything acted as if she were made of glass. She did feel a twinge of fear whenever she passed by the places that reminded her of Volker, like the principal's office or the auditorium. But on the whole, she thought she was holding up rather well. Best of all, the busy school seemed to have quieted the nagging voices in her skull.

She brushed her hair away from her face and stared out across the schoolyard. The grass was still brown, and the trees were still bare, but it was much warmer that it had been in weeks. People called it the January thaw. Sometimes it lasted long enough that the trees started budding and a few flowers poked their heads out of the dirt.

But it always got cold again. Sometime in the next couple of weeks, a cold front would come barreling into town and the snow and freezing weather would be back. Talli hugged her books against her and hoped that the despair she'd felt through the holidays wouldn't come back with the snow.

She was about to turn and go back inside, when she spotted the guy she had seen outside her house. He was sitting on the steps, talking to Casey Pays. This time Talli didn't feel as scared, and the voices didn't start their chattering in her head. He looked like a regular guy. And Casey was smiling at him, which proved that he couldn't be a jerk.

A bell sounded inside the school. The students who had been eating outside started gathering up their trays. Talli turned back into the crowded school and headed for her next class. She struggled through the flow and managed to snag a desk near the front of the classroom.

A dark-haired girl stepped into the classroom with her arms full of books. Talli instantly recognized her as the girl who'd been driving the green Dodge the day before. Talli expected the girl to take a seat with the other students, but instead she walked to the front of the room and stood behind the teacher's desk. She dropped her books on the desk and gave the class a bright smile.

"Good afternoon," she said. "I'm—" The second bell sounded, cutting off her words. She waited until the bell had stopped, and the noise in the room had died down, to finish. "I'm Ms. Delany," she said, "your substitute teacher. Ms. Barkawitz isn't going to be returning this year.

I'll be taking over her history classes."

Several of the guys in the back of the room gave low whistles, and there was a ripple of laughter. Ms. Delany ignored it and went on. "I'll also be taking over the drama club. There's a meeting in the auditorium right after school today. So stick around if you're interested."

"Suddenly, I'm interested," whispered the guy seated behind Talli.

A chill went down Talli's back at the mention of the drama club. The auditorium was the scene of many of the things that had happened with Volker. Could it be a coincidence that this stranger in town was taking over in the auditorium?

"Any questions?" asked Ms. Delany.

"Yeah," said the guy behind Talli. "I think I might need some extra study help. How about you give me your phone number?"

The classroom was swept with laughter. Ms. Delany waited for quiet, the smile still on her face. When the last giggles had faded away, she walked slowly around her desk and leaned back against its metal side.

"I agree that you need to work harder, Mr. Hardison," she said. "I've seen your records. I've also seen that you have a history of reprimands. Oh, and I know *your* phone number, and your address." She tapped a finger against her smooth forehead. "I have a photographic memory, Mr. Hardison. I remember everything I read."

The smile faded from her face. "I also remember people who cause me problems, Mr. Hardison," she continued. "Do I make myself clear?"

Talli turned around and saw that the guy was squirming in his seat. "Uh, yeah," he said softly. "I guess so."

"Good," Ms. Delany said. She walked back around the desk, and when she turned again to face the class, her smile was back in place. "Now, I believe that today we're supposed to begin our study of the Civil Rights Movement."

Talli stared at the new teacher with admiration. In two minutes, without raising her voice or making a threat, this small woman had backed down a guy twice her size. Five minutes later Talli's admiration had soared even higher. Ms. Delany was not only capable of handling the class, she was a great teacher.

She moved around the room, bringing the history she was talking about home to the students. She spoke with so much emotion, and brought out so many details, that it was as if she were bringing the past back to life.

When the bell rang, there were groans from half the class. For the first time that Talli could remember, people didn't fly out of the room. They picked up their books slowly and left the room talking about the lesson. Talli was one of the last to leave.

On her way out she stopped by the teacher's desk. "I really enjoyed the lesson," Talli said.

Ms. Delany looked up from the papers on her desk. "Thank you, Ms. McAlister. Will you be at the drama-club meeting?"

Talli was startled. "How did you know my name?"

The teacher thumped the cover of a school yearbook that was lying on her desk. "The same way I knew Mr. Hardison's name. I looked at your pictures in the book."

"You really have that good a memory?" Talli asked.

"Usually," Ms. Delany said with a smile. "Though I can never remember where I put my car keys. Anyway, I do hope you'll be at the drama-club meeting. I've got a project in mind that I think might interest you."

"Okay," said Talli. She returned the teacher's smile with a nervous smile of her own. "I'll see you there."

As Talli walked out of the room, her mind was divided—and it had nothing to do with the voices that whispered inside her skull. The talk of the drama department, and of a special project for Talli, brought back her fears that Ms. Delany had something to do with Volker, that she was one of Them. On the other hand, she seemed so sincere.

Talli found herself wishing that her other classes were already over so that she could talk with Ms. Delany some more. Good or bad, she had to find out what was going on. *I've got to stop worrying about everyone new who comes to town,* she thought. *So Ms. Delany hasn't lived here all her life. That doesn't mean she's a monster. Does it?*

Six

Alex groaned and opened his eyes. The inside of the car was wonderfully dark, but the hillside outside was still being blasted by the late-afternoon sun. Even the light reflected from the ground scorched Alex like the heat from a furnace. He moaned again and shifted his position in the crumpled car.

He understood what had happened—or at least he thought he did. Repairing the injuries he'd gotten in the crash had taken all his energy, drained every spark of life he'd stored up from feeding. When the sun came up, he had no power left to fight it. Alex closed his eyes and tried to return to his uneasy sleep until darkness fell.

A car door slammed. Alex's eyes flew open as he heard someone climbing down the stony hillside toward his hiding place. A pair of boots appeared, framed by the twisted metal of the car window. They were men's cowboy boots, with an elaborate pattern stitched on their brown leather sides.

Alex growled softly. He couldn't afford to be discovered. Not yet. Darkness was drawing closer. If he could hold out for a little while longer, he could crawl from under the car and go looking for someone to feed on. But if he left the car now, the sun might kill him before he could find another place to hide.

From somewhere up the hill, a woman's voice called something that Alex could not understand. "I can't tell," yelled the man standing beside the car. "Doesn't look like anyone's been down here."

A knee and a hand came into Alex's field of view as the man knelt beside the upside-down car. Alex pulled himself as far back into the darkness as he could. He caught a glimpse of a short black beard before he closed his eyes and tried to look dead.

The man muttered something under his breath; then there was a patter of rocks against the side of the car as he stood up. "There's someone inside!" he shouted.

"Are they alive?" asked the woman at the top of the hill.

"I can't tell," the man said again. "We're going to have to call an ambulance."

Yes, thought Alex. *Leave. Go call an ambulance. By the time you get back, it'll be dark, and I'll be gone.*

The man took a few more steps up the slope. Alex could hear his boots scraping on the stony ground. "Mary, you better drive on down to the store on Cabin Road. You can call the police and an ambulance from there."

"Can't you come?" asked the woman. "What are you going to do?"

"I'm going to stay here and see if I can get them out of the car."

A door slammed again, and Alex heard a car speeding off down the highway. He growled again, far down in his throat. His hands tightened their grip on the tattered passenger seat. He watched the man's boots come back toward the wrecked car.

There was a grinding squeal of metal as the man tried to open the car door. He grunted and strained for several long seconds, but the door wouldn't open beyond a tiny crack.

The toes of his boots came so near that Alex could easily have reached out and touched them. Over everything else, he was painfully aware of the bright, pulsing energy that flowed through the man. Alex was so hungry. His body screamed with the need for energy.

Suddenly the level of sunlight outside the car dropped as the sun fell below the pine trees to the west. Relief swept over Alex. Not only did the painful light cease, but it seemed that his brain began to work better. He felt instantly stronger and quicker.

The man outside the car braced one of his boots against a dented fender and pulled at the door again. Something popped, and the door opened with a scream of tortured metal.

Alex looked up to see the man squinting into the dimly lit interior of the car. He was older than Alex had expected, with a lean face and a tight net of wrinkles at the corners of his washed-out gray eyes. He spotted Alex and leaned in. "Are you awake?" he said.

"Yes," Alex said. "I'm hurt. Help me."

"Don't worry, son," the man said. "I'll do what I can."

He reached in. Alex's hands flashed out, and he grabbed the man by the wrist. With one sharp jerk he pulled the man off his feet and into the car. The man shouted as he fell, but there was no one left to hear him.

Then the energy began to flow. The man might be old, but he was full of energy. Alex pulled and pulled, letting the power fill his tired body. When the man held nothing but the fading embers of his life, Alex thrust him aside and climbed out of the wrecked car.

Though his wounds had healed, his clothes hung in tatters. With his jeans and shirt torn to shreds, he felt like a scarecrow that had been left in the fields over winter.

The sun had set, but it was still hours away from full dark. Alex breathed in the evening air. He heard his latest victim moan and roll over in the wreck. The hunger rose in Alex, pushing him to go back and take the last ounce of energy from the man, but Alex resisted.

He shied back against the wreck as the lights of a car came around a curve on the road above. The car pulled over to the side of the road, and again Alex heard a car door slam as a woman got out. She walked through the glare of the headlights, casting her shadow far down the slope, and stood at the edge of the hill.

"Henry?" called the woman.

To Alex the woman looked like a beacon in the darkness. She was filled with energy, energy he needed badly. If only he could find a way to get close to her.

"Henry?" she called again. "You all right?"

Alex glanced down at the man in the wreck. He wondered whether the woman would realize he wasn't Henry if he walked up the hill in the dim light.

A strange feeling came over Alex. It was as if his bones had suddenly gone soft. He leaned against the wrecked car as the sensation spread out to his skin, like an army of electric ants marching over every inch of his body.

When it was over, Alex felt different. He raised a hand to his face and was surprised to feel the bristles of a beard under his palm. He leaned down to the wreck and looked into the twisted sideview mirror. He saw his own eyes peering out of Henry's face.

"Henry!" the woman shouted. "Do you hear me? I called the police. Somebody'll be out here in just a minute."

Alex stood and began to walk up the hill. The woman looked down at him. "Is that you, Henry?"

"Yes," said Alex. It was dark enough now that his vision had changed. He saw the woman in shades of light that came from her own heat.

She was frowning, trying hard to see down the darkened hill. "Henry?" she said again. She sounded worried and confused. As Alex came closer, her features became tight with fear. "What happened to your clothes?" she asked. "Are you okay?"

"I'm fine," said Alex. He walked through the gap that the car had made in the guardrail and stood in front of the woman.

She backed away from him. "What happened to you?" she asked.

"Come here," said Alex.

The woman shook her head. "There's something wrong. What's wrong, Henry?"

"I'm just tired," said Alex. "Tired and hungry. I tore my clothes trying to get into that car. I'm sorry if I scared you."

The woman's features softened, and she stepped closer to Alex. "You did scare me," she said.

"Sorry," Alex said again. He reached out to the woman, and she took his hand. He pulled her close.

She shivered as he began to drain the precious energy from her body. By the time the police arrived, she was lying unconscious on the side of the road.

Alex was long gone.

Seven

Chris ran his finger over the leather spines of the books as he walked down the aisle. He stopped when he reached Dashiell Hammett. After a bout of reading Agatha Christie's upper-class novels, a dash of Hammett's down-and-dirty realism seemed the right thing to Chris. He pulled down a copy of *The Dain Curse* and glanced at the text on the cover.

"You done yet?"

Chris turned to see Casey waiting at the end of the aisle. "Almost," he said. "There's something else I want to check on before we go."

"If I'd known you were going to take this long," Casey said, "I wouldn't have offered you a ride." Chris started to protest, but Casey broke into her characteristic grin. "Only kidding," she said with a shrug. "I don't have any big plans for tonight."

Clutching his book, Chris headed back to the main desk. The librarian, an older woman with glasses that hung from a chain around her neck, looked up at Chris. "Do you have a library card?" she asked.

He shook his head. "No. I need to apply for one."

"To get a card, you have to be a local resident," said the librarian. "Do you have proof of residency?"

"Well—"

Casey stepped forward. "He just moved in, Ms. James. His family bought the house where the Deverauxs used to live."

The librarian pursed her lips and looked from Casey, to Chris, and back to Casey. "All right, Ms. Pays." She shook a bony finger. "But it's on your head if this book isn't returned."

Chris filled out the information for a card with Casey helping him get his new address correct. He handed it over to the librarian, and she carefully lettered his name on a piece of blue cardboard. "Just keep this till your card comes in the mail," she said.

"Thanks," Chris said. "There was something else I was wondering. Do you have a newspaper morgue?"

"Morgue?" Casey asked. "Isn't that where they keep dead people?"

"And dead newspapers," Chris said. He

turned back to the librarian. "Do you keep back issues of the local paper?"

"We keep them on hand for one month," she replied. "After that, we send them out to have them put on microfilm."

"Excuse me a second." Chris took Casey by the arm and steered her back between two stacks of books.

"What are you doing, Chicago?" asked Casey. "Are you nuts or something?"

"When did the disappearances happen?" Chris asked.

"What?"

"All the people that disappeared. When did it happen?"

Casey rolled her eyes up in thought. "In November, I guess. Before Thanksgiving, and after Halloween."

"Okay, thanks." Chris started to walk away, but this time Casey grabbed his arm.

"Wait a minute," she asked. "What are you trying to do?"

"I'm trying to figure out what happened here," Chris said. "If I look at the old newspapers, maybe I'll get a better idea of what went on."

Casey narrowed her blue eyes. "Playing detective, huh, Chicago? Why?"

Chris ignored her question. He wasn't exactly sure why he wanted to find the answers to all the unanswered questions floating around Westerberg. Maybe it was the frustration of not being able to find out anything about his parents' murderer. In the detective novels he loved, the world was so simple. Sherlock Holmes and Miss Marple always figured out who did it. Just once Chris wanted the real world to be like that—every issue tied up with no loose ends. He headed back to the desk.

"Do you have the microfilm for November?" he asked the librarian.

"It's in the drawers," she said. She got up from her desk and showed Chris where to find the film. She also showed him how to load it onto the machine.

Chris already knew how, but he didn't interrupt. "Thank you," he said when she was finished. The librarian went back to her desk, while Casey pulled up another chair and looked over Chris's shoulder.

The image on the screen was a reverse white-on-black view of the local paper. It showed that the *Westerberg Leader* was similar to every other small-town paper that Chris had seen. Stories of parades and local events were crowded on the front page. Real news was left for the inside. The paper was weekly, with dates that went from one Wednesday to the next. He scrolled through the pages of the first November issue without finding anything. He started into the second one and was halfway through it without any luck.

"Wait a sec," said Casey. She pointed at the

screen. "Right there. That's where Mr. Shay, the old principal, left the school, and Mr. Volker took over as principal."

Chris scanned the article quickly. "It doesn't say anything there about Shay disappearing. It says he left town unexpectedly and resigned his position as principal."

"That's what everybody thought," Casey said. "It was weeks before someone came around looking for him. Then people couldn't remember who it was that said he was leaving."

There was nothing else of interest in that week's paper. The next paper was different. The front page still carried an article on upcoming plans for a Thanksgiving parade, and accounts of a record November snowfall. But from the second page on, the paper was filled with articles on missing children.

Chris again saw the pretty face of the missing Samantha Deveraux. Flanking her photo were others whose names were unfamiliar to him.

Casey pointed to the reverse image of a girl with a roundish face and dark hair. "That's Lisa Taylor," she said. "She was Talli's best friend." Her finger moved across the screen to a smiling boy with a football helmet under his arm. "And that's Alex Cole, Talli's boyfriend."

Chris slid a notebook from his backpack and turned to a clean page. He wrote the name of each missing student on a line, along with the date they had vanished. Casey continued to point out each face, adding a few comments about what the students had been like.

"Okay," Chris said when he had finished making his list. "So, looking at them all at the same time, do you see anything?"

"Like what?" Casey asked.

"Like a pattern. Do you see any connection between them? Were they all friends?"

Casey shook her head sharply. "No way. Lisa and Alex were probably friends, but neither of them was part of Samantha Deveraux's little clique. And this bunch"—she pointed to a group of boys—"they were all real jerks. I don't think they had anything to do with the others."

"They weren't all involved in the same sports? Clubs? Related in some way?" Casey shook her head to every question. "Okay," said Chris. "Now we go on with the rest of the paper."

"Why?" Casey asked.

"To see what else happened in town that week," Chris replied. "If the clues aren't in who was missing, maybe they're in something else."

"How do you know there are clues?"

"There are always clues."

"I think you've been reading too many mystery novels," Casey said. "There's no guarantee that you'll find anything."

"Not if I don't look," Chris said. He went back to the first page and looked again at all the innocuous articles. The truth was, he had no idea what he was looking for, but these old papers were his only window into the disappearances.

Two pages after the article about the missing students, he came across the article on Principal Henry Volker. "No picture," said Chris.

Casey shrugged. "As far as I know, he was only in town for a week."

Chris jotted another note on his pad. "Who got Volker his job? Was he appointed by the board?"

"I don't know. He just came in when Shay left."

He looked a bit longer at the article on Volker, but there was no information to suggest what might have happened to the principal. "Okay, let's go on."

The rest of the paper seemed empty of anything related to the missing kids. Chris went on to the next week's paper.

There was another article. This time the disappearance of Volker was grouped together with the other disappearances. There were quite a few quotes from local officials who were speculating on what had happened. Most thought that Volker was somehow tied in with some drug arrests that had taken place at the school. Others thought that Volker might have been killed by those same drug dealers.

Chris scanned the rest of that week's paper, and into the following weeks. There were more articles, but with each week they grew smaller, and the amount of new information decreased. He looked up at Casey. "Well," he said. "There's one thing that's clear."

"Which is?" she asked.

"As soon as Volker was gone, the disappearances stopped."

"So you think Volker was involved," Casey said.

"Yes," Chris said slowly. "I do." He spun the dial on the microfilm machine and turned back to the second article on Volker's disappearance. "Look here," he said, gesturing at the screen. "In Volker's house they found very little furniture, but many boxes of clothing."

Casey tapped the screen. "Yeah, but none of the clothing matched the missing people."

"Still, it's a strange thing for a high-school principal to be carting around," Chris said. "There's nothing in here about a wife or anything, but a lot of the clothes were women's clothes, or kids'." He tapped his pencil against the screen. "This Volker, he was up to something. He comes into town, Shay disappears. Volker takes over as principal, but did you notice there was no mention of a school-board meeting, or any announcement? Volker stays only a little over a week, but in that week a bunch of people disappear."

He looked up at Casey. "And there was one other thing in the paper the week Volker was in town. Something very interesting. Did you notice?"

She shook her head. "No, I was just reading the articles." She reached past him and turned the dial. For several minutes she moved back and forth over the pages, but at last she shook her head. "All right, Sherlock, I give up. What was special about that paper?"

Chris put his hand over Casey's and slowly turned the dial forward a few pages to the obituaries. "Right there," he said. "The week Volker was in town, there were more than twice as many deaths in Westerberg as either the week before or the week after."

Laughter greeted Talli as she walked into the auditorium. The front two rows were nearly full of students. It was a higher attendance than Talli had ever seen for a drama-club meeting. As she walked down the sloping aisle and found a seat near the back of the group, she also noted how many guys there were in the crowd. Usually the drama club had to be careful to pick plays that had lots of female roles, because they couldn't get enough guys to be in the plays. Today there were enough guys in the auditorium to put on a play about the army. And it wasn't hard to tell why—every one of them had his eyes firmly fixed on the dark-haired teacher in the front of the room.

Other teachers had trouble working in the

auditorium. The huge space seemed to swallow them up. Ms. Delany had no trouble. She moved around the foot of the stage as enthusiastically as she had in her classroom. Her voice seemed quite capable of carrying the length of the room.

Talli relaxed in the padded chair. Memories of the monster that had chased her through the dark theater faded. With the lights on, and plenty of people there, the auditorium didn't seem like a terrible place at all.

"All right," Ms. Delany said. "I think it's decided that we will stage three productions this spring. That's almost one a month, and I don't mind telling you that it means a lot of work." She shook her finger at the boys in the front row. "And that means that every one of you will be expected to come back. If you're not going to help, now is the time to leave."

She waited a moment, but not one guy moved. "Right. Now, the only question is, what plays do we plan on presenting?"

Marcia Malone, a blond girl who had played the lead in many of the club's productions, raised her hand and stood when Ms. Delany pointed in her direction. "It seems like we're always doing old things," Marcia said. "I mean, like Shakespeare and stuff." There was a ripple of laughter and the girl looked around her with a scowl. Marcia had always been a very upbeat person, and a friend of both Talli's and Alex's.

But her brother had been one of the people who vanished. Since then Marcia's temperament had grown thorny.

"All I know is, it would be nice to do something that people want to see," she said. "Why can't we do one of the plays that people are talking about on TV?" She sat down quickly.

Ms. Delany looked thoughtful. "There are difficulties with putting on something that's too new, Ms. Malone. For example, the plays that are currently in production on Broadway, or touring the country, are generally not available for amateur productions. Another problem is that some of them have very elaborate staging, which would be difficult for us to reproduce."

She walked up the aisle and stood beside the blond girl. "But I think you may have an idea," Ms. Delany continued. "I think we should still do at least one classic work." There was a soft groan from several people, but Ms. Delany kept going. "I believe you'll find that there are a number of people who are interested in works like those of Shakespeare."

Marcia's frown grew deeper. "Not me," she muttered.

Ms. Delany put her hand on the girl's arm. "The news isn't all bad," she said. "Did you know that many of the plays that are popular today are revisions or revivals of older works?

For example, *The Phantom of the Opera* is based on an older work."

Marcia's face brightened. "Could we do that?"

"Maybe," Ms. Delany said, "or another work that would catch the public's eye." She walked back toward the front of the auditorium. "I think we've just about selected our first two productions." She held up her fingers and ticked them off. "We'll do one classic work, and one more recent work."

"What about the other one?" asked a guy in the front row. "You said there would be three."

Ms. Delany smiled. "For the third production I have something special in mind." Her eyes seemed to search the audience until they found Talli. "Ms. McAlister, I'm glad to see you here."

Talli straightened in her chair. She didn't know what to say, but the scrutiny of everyone in the room made her very uncomfortable.

"Didn't you win the short-fiction contest two years back, Ms. McAlister?"

"Yes," said Talli. "When I was a sophomore."

"In fact," Ms. Delany said, "your story won third place in the state, didn't it?"

Talli nodded again. "But it wasn't that good."

Ms. Delany reached for a pile of papers stacked on one of the chairs and pulled off a manila folder. "You're being too modest," she said. "I've read the story, and it's very good."

"Um, thanks," said Talli. She was blushing furiously, and she didn't understand why Ms. Delany was bringing this up in front of everybody.

The teacher walked up the aisle to Talli with the folder tucked under her arm. "For our third production," she said, "I'd like to try something very special." She stopped and looked down at Talli. "Tell me, Ms. McAlister, have you ever thought about writing a play?"

Talli had to clear her throat before she could answer. "No," she said. "I don't know how to write a play."

"I hope you're willing to learn," said Ms. Delany. "For our last production of the year, I'd like to present an original play." The smile was still on her face, but her brown eyes looked very serious. "And I'd like you to write it, Talli," she said softly. "Will you try?"

Talli licked her lips. She hadn't tried to write anything in months, but she could still remember how wonderful it had felt when her story won the contest. "Okay," she said. "If you'll help me."

"Don't worry," Ms. Delany said. "I'll make sure you get all the help you need."

She turned back to the rest of the group and started giving them suggestions on the first two plays. Talli was left sitting in her chair with her heart beating so loudly, it seemed to have moved into her ears.

Can I really write a whole play? she wondered. *What will I write about?*

At the front of the room, people were shouting the names of recent movies and plays that had come from older works. "Let's do something with some action," suggested one boy. "Why not something about the environment?" asked another.

Talli pulled out a notebook as the discussion rolled on. She held her pen over the paper, trying to think of anything to write about. She had been telling the truth—it had been a long time since she'd tried to write anything. Writing something that would be seen by the whole school sounded next to impossible.

I need a good idea, she thought. *If I only had one good idea, then I could write something*.

"I've got it!" shouted a girl in the front row. "Let's do Dracula."

Talli looked up quickly. She felt as if she had been slapped in the face. Other students were making suggestions, but Talli didn't hear them. That girl had given her all the ideas she needed.

"Write about a vampire," she said under her breath. Then she leaned over her pad and began to make notes.

Eight

"There's been an accident," said Alex. "Can I come in and use the phone?"

The woman blinked at him and looked down at his tattered clothes. She was an old woman, with a tight cap of white curls and thick round glasses. "My husband isn't here right now," she said. "I'm not sure I should let you in."

Alex tried to put more desperation into his voice. "It'll just take a second," he said. "Please? My friend is still in the car. She's hurt really bad."

The woman frowned and looked past him down the dark road. "I don't know," she said. Her eyes scanned Alex's clothing again. He knew he certainly looked as if he had been in an accident. "Come on in," she said at last. "I'll show you the phone."

Alex followed her through the door and into the kitchen. It felt strange to be inside a house. He had frequently hidden in sheds or abandoned buildings, but he couldn't remember the last time he had been in a house. Usually he got a very bad feeling whenever he went near a home.

"Here's the phone," said the woman. A nervous smile came to her round face. "I'm sorry I didn't let you in right away."

"That's all right," Alex said. "You can't be too careful these days."

He reached out and took her by the neck. The expression on her face barely had time to change from a smile to surprise before she was unconscious.

Alex laid the woman carefully on the kitchen floor and left the phone dangling from its hook. He walked through the living room, leaving muddy footprints on the carpet, and headed for the stairs. He hadn't needed the woman to tell him that there was no one else in the house—his night vision showed him that. But he was very glad to hear that she had a husband, because what he needed most was clothing.

Alex searched two closets before he found the right one. Taking off his own shredded sweater and jeans, he dropped them on the floor. From the closet Alex pulled a pair of dark new jeans and a plaid shirt of heavy flannel.

The fit wasn't perfect, but at least it was good enough for him to pass people without drawing too much attention.

Alex walked over to the dresser in the corner of the room and stared into the mirror. His face seemed the same as usual, except for the dirt that stained it. He concentrated, trying to get back the feeling that had come to him at the wreck. At first there was no change; then the sensation of crawling ants came back. In a matter of seconds the face in the mirror thinned and lengthened. A dark beard sprouted and grew so quickly, it seemed to pour from his skin like a liquid.

The change was not restricted to his face. The clothing, which had been big to begin with, now hung loose over a thinner, rangier frame. Alex lifted a hand to his face and looked at the long, bony fingers. He wondered how far the change could go. Could he change into the shape of someone he had seen only in a picture, or did it have to be someone he had fed from? Could he change into the form of someone very different from himself—like a woman?

He relaxed, and there was an audible hum as his face and body reshaped themselves into his normal form. It didn't matter, he decided. Even if this new ability was limited, it would give him access to life. He could go anywhere and not have to worry about being recognized.

Alex left the bedroom and went back downstairs. The woman was still unconscious on the kitchen floor. From what he had seen in the past, Alex figured that it would be hours before her body replaced enough of the stolen energy for her to get up. He stepped over her and looked around the room, trying to see if there was anything else he needed.

The kitchen was well stocked with food, but even the smell of it made Alex feel vaguely sick. There were knives there, too, but Alex didn't need any weapons except his own hands. Then he spotted the car keys on the counter. He hadn't even thought of taking a car, but now that the keys were in front of him, it seemed like a perfect idea.

Alex picked up the keys and let them dangle from his hand as he went in search of the car. The garage was dark, but Alex had no trouble seeing. The car was large and old, with spots of rust showing above the rear wheels. That didn't matter—Alex wasn't out to impress anyone. He climbed inside and shoved the key into the ignition.

He couldn't remember the last time he had driven a car. Like everything else in his past, it was lost in a kind of fog. He didn't think he would have any trouble remembering how to drive. The actions came very easily as he settled himself in the seat and cranked the engine.

The engine roared to life. Alex backed out of the dark garage. It had begun to rain, and it took him a few seconds to find the wipers before he continued down the slick black highway.

His driving was cautious at first, but soon he was going far above the speed limit. Not only did he remember how to drive, but his new senses seemed to connect him to the car better than ever before.

A sign came up on the right side of the road. Alex slammed on the brakes, bringing the car to a skidding halt.

WESTERBERG 50, said the sign.

Westerberg again. There was something about that name that both excited and frightened Alex. If he went there, he was certain something would happen. But he had no idea what.

He pressed on the gas, and the old car rumbled off through the rain. Alex was halfway to Westerberg before he remembered to turn on the headlights.

Nine

Tuesday

Chris missed the cereal bowl with his spoon and left a trail of milk across the table. He dropped the spoon and rubbed his eyes. He might get used to a lot of things while living in Westerberg, but he didn't think that getting up at dawn was going to be one of them.

His sister put a glass of orange juice by Chris's elbow as she whirled around the table and dropped into her own chair. As usual, Donna looked ready for anything. "You didn't talk much last night," she said. "What did you think of your first day in Westerberg?"

"It was . . . interesting," said Chris.

"Uh-oh. You sound like someone describing a really, really bad date."

"It wasn't so bad," he replied. "I meant it when I said it was interesting. The school wasn't how I pictured a small-town school." He picked up his juice and took a sip.

"What do you mean?" asked Donna. "Did you expect all the kids to wear overalls and bring goats with them to class?"

Chris choked on his juice as he laughed. "No," he said, wiping his mouth. "I guess not. I just didn't expect it to be so crowded and so loud. It was more like going to school in the middle of a city than in a small town."

Donna nodded. "I have to admit that I was a bit disturbed by the number of kids in each class. The school board certainly didn't say anything about fifty kids in a class when they hired me!" She drank her glass of juice in one long swallow and hurried out of the room.

Chris rubbed again at his sleep-matted eyes. He leaned back in his chair and yawned. He had decided that he would try to get ready in time to drive in with Donna this morning. He liked the idea of running into Talli McAlister again if he walked, but it was gray and overcast outside, and he didn't really feel like hiking two miles in the rain.

Donna came striding back into the room with her briefcase in her hand. She sat down at the table with a frown. "I don't think it went too well yesterday."

Chris almost choked on his juice again. "Are

you kidding? Everyone I met asked me if I was related to that great new teacher." He shook his head in amazement. "When are you ever going to give yourself a break and realize that you do a terrific job at everything?"

Donna wrinkled her small nose. "Still, it didn't go like I wanted it to. After the day was over, I thought of a hundred things that happened that I could have handled better."

"Yeah, well, there's the problem with that perfect memory," Chris said. "It won't let you alone."

Donna smiled. "There was one thing that went really well, though."

Chris picked up his spoon. "What's that?" he asked as he started in again on his soggy cereal.

"There's a girl in one of my classes who's really been troubled. The school counselor talked to me about it yesterday morning. He thought since I was the drama coach, I might think of something to pull her out of her shell."

"And you did?" Chris asked.

"Absolutely." Donna leaned far back in her chair and put her hands behind her head. "I looked through her records and found out that she won an award for her writing. She also happened to be involved with the drama club. So I asked her to write a play that the drama club will produce."

"Pretty slick, sis," Chris said. "You think she'll come through?"

"I know she will. She just needs something to put her back on track." Donna grabbed the cereal box and stuck her hand down through the top. She came out with a fistful of shredded-wheat squares and started munching them.

"Don't do that," Chris moaned.

His sister lowered her eyebrows and scowled at him with mock severity. "Don't correct the teacher," she said. "I might have to put you in detention."

"You wouldn't do that," Chris said.

"And why not?"

"Because if you did," he replied, "you'd have to unpack all the stuff from the moving van yourself when it shows up this afternoon."

"Good point." Donna got up and brushed the crumbs from her hands. "Okay, I'll let you slide this time. But you'd better watch it in the future. Now, if you want a ride, get your shoes on so we can go."

Chris shoveled in a few more quick spoonfuls of cereal, then he hurried to find his coat and shoes so he could meet Donna at the door. She was waiting for him with the front door already open, fumbling through her purse. Finally she looked up in frustration.

"I don't suppose you know where the car keys are?" she asked with a sigh.

He held up his hand, letting the keys dangle from his finger. "You left them on the counter in the bathroom. I spotted them this morning."

"Thanks," she said as she took them and headed through the door.

Chris turned the dial on the back of the knob, locking the door as he closed it. "You know, you ought to do something about that thing with the keys," he called after Donna. "You've got a real mental block."

Donna didn't answer as Chris followed her to the car. Ten seconds after she pulled the Dodge out of the driveway, the clouds opened up, and a cold rain began to fall. Chris shivered. He was glad he had decided to take the ride.

"Who was the girl?" he asked as they moved down the wet streets.

"What girl?"

"The one you asked to write a play."

"Oh," Donna said. "I'm not sure I should tell you that. She's had a really hard time. A lot of her friends were in the group of kids that disappeared."

Chris turned to look at his sister. "Is it Talli McAlister?" he asked.

Donna glanced over at him in surprise, then turned her attention back to the road. "How did you know that?" she asked. "Did you see us talking?"

Chris grinned at her. "A great detective has ways of finding out these things."

At the next stoplight Donna twisted around in her seat and stared at him. "You like Talli, don't you?" she asked.

"What do you mean?" Chris asked. "I haven't even met her."

Donna arched an eyebrow. "I've been your big sister for seventeen years now," she said. "Big sisters know *more* than great detectives." She stepped on the gas, and the car headed into downtown Westerberg.

Chris stared down at his feet and frowned. "It's strange," he said after a few seconds. "I've never met her, but I do like her." He shrugged. "There's something about her that makes me want to get close to her."

"See. Big sister is always right." The single stoplight in the center of town was red, and Donna turned to him again as they waited for it to change. "Listen, Chris, I think it's great that you like Talli. I've only talked to her a little, but she seems like a really nice girl." She held up a finger to stop Chris's reply. "Remember, she's been hurt badly. Don't do anything to make it worse, okay?"

"Sure," Chris said. "I don't want to hurt her."

Donna had a reserved parking spot close to the school, but Chris was still thoroughly cold and damp by the time he got inside. It was strange being in the school so early. The halls that had been so crowded the day before were empty, and it was so quiet that his footsteps echoed through the building.

Chris went to his locker and put away most of his things, getting out the books he would need for the first couple of periods. After that he still had almost an hour to kill before it was time for school to start. He sat in his first classroom for a while, trying to work up enthusiasm for the lessons that had been assigned the day before. But again and again his mind kept drifting back to the things he had learned in the library.

Volker had come to the school as principal, and the disappearances had started soon after that. Chris knew he would have to visit the library again and look at the papers more closely. There were bound to be other things that had happened, things that had seemed unrelated at the time, which were clues to where the missing students had gone.

He wondered if the school building itself might hide some clues to the mystery. Surely, a great detective ought to be able to find something. With that thought in mind, he got up from his desk and began wandering through the hallways.

A few students had started to arrive, but the school was still almost empty. Chris paused and looked at the walls. The paint seemed fresh—it looked as if the school had been repainted over the Christmas holidays. Was that a clue? Or did it just mean the school had needed painting? Chris had no idea, but he filed it away with everything else.

The principal's office was open. The secretary, a stocky woman with thick glasses, was bent over a bulky stack of files. Chris leaned back against the wall and looked through the door of the inner office. There he could see the new principal, also a woman, talking on the phone. This was another thing he'd have to check out. How did the school board come up with a third principal after Volker disappeared?

Chris walked on down the hall to the double doors at the top of the auditorium. He pushed through the doors and found himself in almost total darkness. The lights were off in the lobby, and only the palest of glows spilled in from the main hall. He stepped forward, feeling the edge of the door to the actual auditorium, and reached for the knob.

The door opened before his fingers could reach it. A dark figure bumped into him, sending him back across the lobby. His heart was beating in his throat as he scrambled to find the door that would let him back into the main hall of the school.

Instead his hand fell on a bank of light switches. Without hesitation, he slammed the switches down.

At once the lobby was filled with blinding white light, leaving Chris staring directly into the terrified eyes of Talli McAlister.

It had taken Talli three tries to work up the

courage to open the auditorium door and step inside. Once in, she had a rush of terror as she thought of the last time she had been alone in this place. She reached out for the padded back of the nearest chair and squeezed. After a few moments the fear began to fade.

The auditorium was just a place. Without Volker to fill it with horror, it was just a big room with a lot of chairs. Talli stepped around the back row of chairs and sat down. She put her notebook on her lap and tried to think of how to form the events of the previous November into a play.

She couldn't use Volker's name, or anyone else's—that much was certain. Talli wasn't sure how close to the real events she could come. On the one hand, it might make people upset. On the other hand, what had really happened was so strange that people wouldn't believe it. They were bound to think that Talli had come up with the whole thing as some kind of horrible fantasy.

She tapped her pencil against the pad. The ideas had flowed rapidly when she first started jotting down notes, but putting a shape to the whole thing was giving her a problem. So was staging. When a story ranged over a whole town, and a lot of what happened involved fighting or chases, how did you get that into a play?

This project wouldn't be easy—Talli wasn't

even convinced that she could do it. But she was determined to stick with it, if only for one reason: from the moment she had started writing, the voices in her head had fallen silent.

Talli heard the muffled sound of a car door slamming outside. She glanced at her watch and saw that it was barely a half hour before school was supposed to start. Writing would have to wait until lunch or free period. She closed her notebook and headed up the sloping aisle toward the lobby.

She was looking over her shoulder at the bare stage as she pushed open the door. Someone was standing in the darkened lobby. At once all the terror that had been hiding down inside her came boiling up. This time she didn't run. She couldn't run. She stood frozen in the darkness, waiting for the death she knew was coming.

Then the lights came on. In the glare she found herself staring at the boy she had seen with Ms. Delany. He looked as frightened as she felt.

"Are you—" he started, his voice a high-pitched squeak. He stopped, cleared his throat, and tried again. "Are you all right?"

Talli nodded quickly. "I'm fine. What are you doing here?"

"I was just looking around," said the boy. "I didn't mean to scare you." He took a step forward and stuck out his hand. "I'm Chris Delany."

Talli hesitated for a moment, then reached out for his hand. "Talli McAlister." She looked down at their linked hands. "You're trembling," she said in surprise.

Chris pulled his hand back. "I guess we scared each other," he said.

Talli looked at him more closely. "You must be Ms. Delany's brother."

He nodded.

"She's a great teacher," Talli said. "I think she's the best teacher I've ever had."

Chris smiled, and Talli was surprised at how much it lit up his face. "She is great," he said, "but she must have really impressed you for you to say that after one day."

Talli shrugged. "I usually have a good feel for people, and my feeling tells me that your sister is something special."

There was an awkward silence. When it had stretched out uncomfortably long, Chris glanced toward the doors that led back into the hallway. "Well, I guess it's about time for school to start," he said.

"We better get moving," Talli said with a nod.

Chris reached for the door, and Talli started past him, but instead of opening the door, Chris turned back to her. "Listen, um . . . I mean . . . I don't suppose that after school, you'd like to go somewhere?"

Talli was taken completely by surprise, and

she simply stared at him, her tongue feeling paralyzed in her mouth.

"Just to talk," he added quickly. "Or maybe we could get something to eat?"

"No," Talli managed to say. "I don't think that would be such a good idea." She pulled the door open.

"Maybe another day?" Chris asked as she stepped past him.

"Maybe," Talli said, desperate to get away. She glanced back as she walked down the hall. Chris was still standing by the auditorium doors. He smiled nervously.

Talli couldn't tell if she smiled back or not. Her whole face felt kind of tingly and numb. She wasn't ready to go out yet. Not yet. It had been over six weeks since Alex had disappeared. Sometimes those six weeks seemed like six years. Sometimes they seemed like six seconds. She had been going out with Alex since she was old enough to date. In fact, Talli had never dated anyone but Alex. The idea of going out with someone else seemed wrong somehow.

She reached her classroom and sat down. There was a tightness in her throat, and tears were welling up in her eyes. Talli brushed them away. She would have to go out with someone else eventually. Life had to go on.

It doesn't have to, said a very dark voice in her mind.

Talli shuddered and put her hands to her head. Then she reached into her backpack, jerked open a notebook, and began to write as fast as she could.

For the rest of that day, she wrote constantly. The teachers must have thought she was taking notes, because none of them stopped her. But it wasn't notes that was filling the pages of Talli's notebook. It was a story of monsters and murder. She wasn't worried about staging anymore. She wasn't worried about what names to use.

She just kept writing. She wrote to keep the voices away.

Ten

Having a car had given Alex the freedom to move as he passed through the dark countryside. In one night he had fed four times.

First there had been the woman whose car he took. Next had come a hitchhiker who was unfortunate enough to be thumbing for a ride where Alex was driving. When the hunger rose up again, Alex parked outside a small store and waited for an unwary customer in the dark parking lot. Then, just before dawn, he pulled over and put some gas in the car. He left the gas-station attendant unconscious in his chair.

Alex knew he should have found a place to sleep by now. The sun was already up, and though it didn't hurt him as it had when he was empty of energy, he could feel it draining his power. He would have stopped if it weren't for the signs telling him that Westerberg was close. With every mile Alex spotted more things that seemed familiar.

Images were floating through his mind—images that he could not put a name to. He passed a wide field carpeted in fallen brown cornstalks. There was no one there, but for a second Alex saw children running through the field towing a kite behind them. He seemed to be among the children. Then the children were gone. Alex turned his head, and for a moment he found himself in the park on the other side of the road with the hard wood of a baseball bat in his hands.

It was too much to handle. For so long he had thought of nothing but the endless hunger—his only goal had been to satisfy it. His past had been hazy, brief, and uncertain, but he always knew what to do next. Like a well-tuned machine, he would get up and do his job. He would feed. Now there was something wrong with the machine.

The wheels of the car grated in the gravel at the side of the road. Alex jerked the wheel back and centered the car on the street, but a moment later he was off the road again. It was no use. The strange images were coming so fast and thick that he could barely see where he was going.

Alex pulled off the road and drove the car slowly across a muddy field. There was a weather-beaten old barn near the center of the field. Alex drove through the doors that gaped open at one end, and stopped. The warped gray walls of the barn let in only tiny slivers of sunlight. Alex sat in the car, his fingers gripping the hard plastic of the steering wheel. Slowly he reached down and turned the key. The car died, leaving the barn in silence.

Out of the sunlight, Alex could think more clearly. The images in his mind had to be memories, he decided. He had other memories—of places where he had hidden through the day, and of people he had fed from.

But when had he ever run through a field with children? Why would he stand out in the daylight like that? Why not drain the energy from the children and leave? The other image, the one of himself holding a baseball bat, brought with it many other memories, enough that Alex could remember that baseball was a . . . game. Why would he be part of something like that? Did it help to satisfy the hunger?

Alex clamped his eyes shut and tried to make sense of these new memories. The strange sensations had started when the man who had given him a ride two nights before had mentioned Westerberg. Now that Alex was so close to Westerberg, more and more memories were coming back. So he must have hidden here in the past. But somehow that didn't seem quite right. Finally the drain of the sunlight slanting through the barn walls became too strong to ignore. Alex crawled into the backseat of the car and lay down on the floorboard. With the strange images still whirling through his mind, he went into his daytime sleep.

On most days Alex fell into darkness and lay still until night. This time something happened that had never happened before. Alex dreamed.

He was in a room with a green metal desk and two folding metal chairs. Everything felt absolutely real, more real than what had happened yesterday, and the day before, as far back as Alex could remember. Alex was sitting in one of the chairs. The other chair lay on its side. He could see every chip in its brown paint. He could feel the cold metal of the chair against his back, and he smelled the peculiar odor of paper and ink that told him he was in an office.

He stared at the fallen chair. Someone had been sitting there. Someone was gone. It was very important, Alex knew, but he had no idea why.

A person came into the room. Alex tried to turn his head, but it was as if his neck were locked in place. A man dressed in a police uniform stepped into view.

"She got away, Principal Volker," said the man, "but we'll catch her."

"Don't worry," said another voice. Suddenly Alex was aware that there was a second man in the room, seated behind the green desk. Until the man spoke, Alex had not seen him. He was a tall, thin man in a gray suit.

The tall man stood, walked over to the policeman, and put a hand on his shoulder. "You've done fine, Sergeant Lansky," he said. "You can go now."

The policeman nodded once and left the room. The tall man eased the door shut and turned to Alex. "Your friend has escaped for the moment," he said. "However, you are still here." He stepped over to Alex and put a long-fingered hand on his cheek. Alex fought to pull away, but he was still frozen, unable to move.

A smile came to the tall man's lips. "Don't fight me, Alex. This will take only a moment, and then you and I will be very, very close." The man moved his hand to Alex's forehead.

At once a painful cold swept over Alex. Darkness welled up and swallowed his vision, and his sense of himself sitting in the chair was lost. The pain and the cold went on and on. At last even the cold was gone, and there seemed to be nothing left but the blackness. Then a brilliant light flared in the dark. Warmth flooded through Alex. With it came strength, and power.

His vision came back, and he saw the tall man looking down at him. "Welcome back, Alex," said Principal Volker. "Welcome to a different world."

Alex woke. He kept his eyes closed for a moment—he didn't want to lose the clarity of the dream. But the dream was fading, slipping away into tatters of color and sound. He climbed up from the backseat and opened the door.

It was dark in the barn. An owl stood on one of the broken doors, staring out into the night. Outside, Alex could hear the soft sound of wind rushing over the winter cornfield. He could see the spots of fire that were animals moving through the night. It was Alex's time.

He walked around the car and slid into the driver's seat. He thought he understood the dream. Like the images that had come over him on the road that morning, the dream came to him out of the past. And if he understood it correctly, it showed that there had been a time Before. Before Volker. A time when the hunger had not driven his life. A time when he had moved around in the daylight and played a game called baseball.

Alex could not imagine a life like that. What was there to do if you did not feed the hunger? Perhaps more images would come, and then he would understand.

He turned the key, but the car didn't start. There was only a faint whine under the hood. Alex didn't try to figure out why the car had stopped running. He just got out and left it.

Alex walked across the muddy field and started up the road toward Westerberg.

Eleven

Wednesday

Casey pulled the notebook across the cafeteria table and looked at the numbers Chris had written. "That many?" she asked.

Chris nodded. "Fourteen," he replied. "That wouldn't be anything in a bigger town, but in Westerberg it's a lot." He tapped his finger on a row of numbers on the notebook. "See here? The average number of deaths in this county is six a week. I went back a whole year to make sure. No other week had more than nine deaths. Then we get to the week Volker was in town, and we get fourteen."

Casey scowled at the paper. "But if you've written all these down right, it doesn't look like anybody was murdered. There's nothing here but accidents, heart attacks, and one suicide."

"I don't know about the accidents, but four of the people who had heart attacks were under forty years old. That seems pretty strange to me. And did you notice who the suicide was?" Chris asked.

"Howard South." Casey looked up from the page. "It sounds kind of familiar."

"His son was Morris South."

Casey wrinkled her nose at the name. "There's one person I don't mind disappearing," she said. "Morris South was a creep. Okay, so his father committed suicide. Maybe he missed his son."

Chris shook his head. "Morris wasn't missing yet. Morris was reported missing by his stepmother, three days after his father died."

"You really are the detective, aren't you?" Casey teased him. She turned back to the notebook. "How long did you stay at the library last night?" she asked as she read.

"Until they threw me out," he said. "There are still some other things I need to check out. I probably should go back today."

Casey's lips moved slightly as she ran her finger across the list of names and dates. "What's this one?" she asked, pointing at an entry on the page.

"Where?"

"Here, where it says 'F. D. Volker.' I thought Volker's first name was Henry."

"Oh, the F.D. stands for fire department," Chris said. "They were called out to Volker's house one Saturday night. It said in the article that someone called in a fire, but there was no one there and no fire."

Casey straightened in her chair and slid the notebook across the table to Chris. "Enough of this stuff," she said. "I happen to know that Talli McAlister is at this moment in the auditorium going over the available props."

"How do you know that?" Chris asked.

Casey stood up and gathered her things. "You aren't the only one who's a great detective, Delany. So, you ready to go meet Talli?"

"We already met."

"What?"

"I ran into her yesterday morning before class," he said. "She was coming out of the auditorium, and I was going in."

"Why didn't you tell me about it when we talked yesterday afternoon?" Casey asked.

Chris smiled. "I didn't want you to be jealous."

"Watch it, Delany," Casey said with a scowl. "I already told you you're not my type."

"Okay." Chris laughed, holding up his hands. "I was only kidding."

Casey shook her head, sending her brown curls flying. "You have a dangerous sense of humor. Anyway, if you want to see Talli, I'm supposed to go in and help her with the scenery."

"Aha," Chris said. "Now we know how you got your information."

"Oh, just come on if you're coming," Casey said. She turned and started down the hall.

Chris hurried to shove his notebook into his backpack and ran down the hall to catch up with Casey at the auditorium doors. She led him through the lobby and down the long slope between the seats. Then they went around the stage and up a flight of stairs that led to a long dim hallway behind the stage.

Chris looked up at the catwalk and cables that faded into the gloom high overhead. "Wow," he said. "*Phantom of the Opera*, here we come."

"Kind of neat, isn't it?" Casey said. "I was in a play last year and I made my entrance from this hall. I've always liked it back here."

The hallway ended at a room filled with racks of clothes, stacks of boxes, and pieces of painted canvas that looked like everything from a paint-spattered alley to the stones of a castle. Talli was not in sight, but there was a lot of thumping and bumping coming from the hidden corners of the room.

"Talli?" Casey called. "Where are you hiding?"

A rack of clothes went sliding away, and Talli stepped out of the clutter. She looked a bit frightened at first, but when she saw Casey, her face brightened.

"Hi," she said, brushing dust from her red hair. "I was trying to get an idea of what's lurking under all this junk."

"I brought someone with me," Casey said. She reached back out to the hall and pulled Chris into the room by his arm. "I think you've already met."

Talli's smile faltered for a moment, but she recovered quickly. "Sure. Hi, Chris."

"Talli," Chris said with a nod. He waved a hand toward the room. "Is there anything I can do to help?"

"There are some trunks in the corner," Talli said. "I haven't been able to get them open."

Chris stepped past Talli and walked to the back of the room. The trunks turned out to be roughly the size of cars, with heavy metal bands along their sides. One of the two was already open a crack. He put his fingers into the gap and heaved, but it didn't budge an inch, so he gave up on the direct approach and scouted around the room. In the corner he found a piece of metal pipe as big around as his thumb and as long as his leg. Armed with this, he attacked the trunk again.

This time the metal hinges opened with an earsplitting squeak. Dust flew up as the top of the trunk fell back with a heavy thud. Chris waved his arms against the clouds of dust. "It's open," he called.

Talli and Casey appeared at his elbow. "We

heard," Casey said dryly. "What's inside?"

Chris squinted into the dark interior of the box. "Hard to tell." He reached in and felt around in the darkness, coming out with a long feathered boa that was missing half its feathers.

Talli took it from him. "Hmm, I don't think this is in fashion anywhere," she said.

Chris reached into the box again and pulled out a battered felt fedora. Casey took it, knocked out the worst of the dents, then shoved it down on Chris's head. "This is just the thing for a great detective," she said.

"Detective?" asked Talli.

"Delany here has been trying to figure out all the things that happened back before Christmas," said Casey. "He thinks he's Sherlock Holmes."

"Well, maybe Sam Spade," said Chris. He turned around, and found Talli looking at him with a very serious expression.

"You're investigating the disappearances," Talli said.

She hadn't said it as if it were a question, but Chris decided to take it that way. "Yes," he said. "I've been looking things up in the papers, mainly."

Talli continued to stare at him without speaking for a long, tense moment. "Good luck," she said at last. Then she nodded toward the open trunk. "Let's see what else you can find in there."

The trunk yielded quite a collection of moldy old props, from a bag that looked like an old doctor's bag, to a corncob pipe almost a foot long. Talli selected the things that she thought were worth saving and had Chris pitch the rest in a stack to throw away.

The trunk was almost empty when the bell rang to signal the end of the period. Chris got up from his knees and brushed the dust off his jeans. "I've got to run," he said.

"Me, too," Casey said. "You all right in here, Talli?"

Talli nodded. "I'm fine. Thanks for the help."

Casey walked quickly out of the room and down the hallway. Chris started out the door after her, then stopped. He pulled the fedora from his head and held it out. "I almost forgot this."

"Keep it," said Talli. "It looks right on you."

He looked at the battered hat, then shoved it back down on his head. "Thanks," he said. "You sure you wouldn't like to go out somewhere? Maybe get something to eat?"

Talli shook her head, but she was smiling. "I don't think it would be such a good idea."

"Okay," Chris said. He turned and started down the hall toward Casey, but he'd gone only a few steps when Talli called out after him.

"Chris!"

He turned and saw her standing in the door of the prop room. "Yeah?"

"Tomorrow night?" she said. "Maybe we could do something then."

"Tomorrow? Sure, that would be great!" Chris called.

"Talk to you tomorrow," Talli said, turning back into the prop room.

Casey smiled as Chris walked down the stairs at the side of the stage. "I knew you two would hit it off," she said.

Talli listed the contents of the trunk on a sheet of paper before she reached up and pulled down the heavy lid. There were enough clothes in the prop room to put fifty people in a play, as long as everyone didn't mind smelling like mothballs.

Unfortunately for Talli, most of the clothes were old. They were better suited for something set fifty years in the past than three months ago. The rest of the props were the same way—it would be a lot easier to put on a play set in Victorian England than in modern Westerberg.

Talli sat back to consider her options. Making a play out of all the events that had really happened would mean having at least a dozen different acts and almost as many sets. There was no way she could do that. The real events had taken place over a week. A lot of cutting would have to be done to fit everything into a play that could last no more than a couple of hours.

Talli pulled out her notebook and forced herself to concentrate. What was the real core of the story? Volker had come to Westerberg. He'd convinced everyone that he could clean up Westerberg High; then he'd used his position to attack the students of the school.

"A stranger," Talli whispered as she wrote, "comes to town. He does something that makes everyone think he is a hero. But he is not a hero. He has come for his own reasons, and he uses his position as a hero to harm the people of the town."

Talli put down her pen. That was the center of what had happened. That it had happened at the school, or that it had happened last November, wasn't important. She would build her play around that one paragraph. After a few seconds of thought, she added one more line. "The people in the town don't realize what is happening until it is too late."

Talli brushed the dust from her legs and gathered her things. She had been sitting in the prop room for a long time, but neither the voices in her head nor the terror the room usually caused her had come back. Talli smiled to herself. Maybe she really would get over what had happened. It had been nice to have Casey come in while she was going through the props. And Chris.

Talli wasn't sure why she had decided to go out with Chris. She liked the way he looked—

even with that silly old hat on his head—and he seemed nice. Casey liked him, and if he was Ms. Delany's brother, he couldn't be too bad. She waited for the voices in her head to make some comment about Chris, but they were silent.

Talli hurried out of the auditorium and made it to her next class just as the bell was ringing. She sat through the lecture and tried to take notes, but her mind kept going back to her play. By the end of the day, she had no idea what any of her teachers had said, but she had filled five pages of her notebook with ideas.

Casey was standing near the door as Talli headed for the parking lot. "You find what you needed in the prop room?" she asked.

"I'm not sure," Talli said. "I may have to ask Ms. Delany if we can make up some new props, but I think we've got most of what I'll need."

"That's good." Casey glanced at her watch. "I'm waiting here for the great detective."

"Chris?"

"Yeah. He decided there was something he wanted to ask the school librarian." She shook her head. "Ten to one he'll want to make another stop at the town library, too."

"He's really working at this, isn't he?" Talli asked. "Why do you think he's so interested?"

"I think you're part of it," Casey said with a grin. "He's been looking to get close to you ever since he hit town. I think that might be what got him started."

"But that's not it now?"

Casey shook her head. "Chris reads a lot of mysteries—maybe too many. I think he's trying to figure it out like one of the detectives in his books. And there's the thing with his parents."

"What about his parents?"

"They were killed," Casey said. "Chris hasn't said too much about it, and I haven't pushed, but they were murdered when he lived in Chicago. I think he's working so hard on this because he couldn't do anything about his parents."

Talli felt uneasy. On the one hand, it was nice that Chris was taking so much interest in the disappearances. If someone else in town had paid attention to things back when they were happening, maybe Volker could have been stopped without so many people dying. On the other hand, if Chris got closer to the problem, he might find out just how involved Talli was. She was the only one who could help him find out what had happened, but she wasn't ready to talk about it.

"Talli?" Casey asked. "Are you all right?"

Talli blinked and realized she had been staring off into space. "Sure. I'm okay."

Casey reached out and put her hand on Talli's arm. "Chris is a really nice guy. I think you two will have fun together."

Talli smiled and headed out to the parking lot. She felt reassured—things were moving forward. Finally she was getting past all the terrible things that had happened. After all, Volker was dead. Talli had seen to that herself. The bad times really were over.

But the sky outside was overcast and gray. A cold front had moved in during the day, and the air was chilly. There was a promise of snow on the way. It reminded Talli of November.

Twelve

The cold didn't bother Alex.

He stood outside the Blue Bird Motel, waiting for his first chance to feed. Most of Westerberg was made up of houses, and houses made it difficult to feed. For some reason, motels didn't seem to generate the kind of discomfort that Alex got when he approached someone's home. The Blue Bird was the only motel in town. A low building with only about twenty rooms, it seemed like a good bet to produce a stranger who wouldn't be missed for a day or two.

He waited in the parking lot, standing in the shadow of a tall van. A family pulled up first, two parents and two kids, with a father carrying one tired child in his arms. Alex considered them. Four people would give a lot of energy, but it also meant four times as much chance that someone would get away, or make a lot of noise. He decided to wait.

When a man in a dark suit and tie pulled up to the office, Alex watched very carefully. He hung back in the shadows until the man had rented a room for the night, then followed him down the row of doors. When the man opened the door, Alex rushed forward, pushed the guy inside, and swung the door closed behind them.

The man was strong. A fist smashed into Alex's face, bringing with it a surprising burst of pain. Furious, Alex grabbed the man by the arm and whirled him across the room. Then he leaped on top of him, pinning the man's arms down. Alex reached out, preparing to feed.

But the man wasn't done. He bucked like a rodeo horse, throwing Alex off. Snatching up a floor lamp from beside the bed, he swung it one-handed, catching Alex in the side.

Alex fell back. The man swung again, and this time the end of the lamp slashed across Alex's face. He felt his skin tear and raised a hand to the wound. Something trickled between his fingers, but it was not the warm flow of blood. It was sparkling energy that oozed through his hand. Brilliant green drops spilled down his face and fell hissing to the carpet.

The man's mouth fell open in astonishment.

He backed away from Alex, the floor lamp raised to deliver another blow. "What are you?" he cried.

Alex could feel the energy fading from his body. He concentrated on the wound and felt again the tingling sensation that came over him when his face changed. The spilling of power from his cheek stopped. With a snarl he jumped for the man.

The lamp thudded hard against his side, but Alex ignored it. His hands locked around his victim's throat, and he lifted until the man's feet dangled above the floor. As Alex began to pull in energy, the guy's kicking became weaker and weaker. The fight had drained Alex, and he pulled hard. Before he knew it, the last spark of energy was gone. The man was dead.

Alex dropped the body onto the motel bed and stepped away. He hadn't meant to drain the man dry. But the fight had left him so hungry. He thought for a moment. Then he walked across the room to the mirror that hung on the wall above the sink.

The place where the floor lamp had torn through his face still showed as a dark red scar. As he looked at it, a line of blue sparks appeared. When they were gone, so was the scar. Alex turned to look back at the body on the bed. The man's face was narrow, with a pointed chin and a long nose. As Alex studied it, the tingling feeling came again to his skin. This time he could see pale-blue lightning spreading over his whole body. He could feel his muscles shifting and his skin flowing.

Alex left the motel room ten minutes later, wearing the man's blue suit. In his pocket was the man's billfold. Inside that were several pictures of a woman that Alex didn't know, but anyone who checked the driver's license would find the face on the card a perfect match to the one Alex was now wearing.

He climbed into the man's shiny new car and pulled out into the road. The streets of Westerberg continued to bring back more and more memories. So far, Alex hadn't been able to fit all these images into any kind of pattern, but he was sure they all had something to do with feeding. Everything in life was about feeding.

A cold rain started to fall, and Alex remembered to turn on the wipers. For the first few minutes he drove around the dark wet streets without any plan other than to find someone else to feed from. He would have to find a place where people were standing outside at night. That would be hard to do, because when it was this cold and wet, people tended to stay home. Westerberg was too small to have the malls and business that lured people out in the dark. Despite all the memories that were coming from the town, Alex thought he would have to leave soon. The hunting here was not good.

He remembered the man who was lying dead back in the hotel room. Alex wasn't sure how he felt about that. He had always tried to stop feeding before the person died, but he didn't really know why. The body was bound to cause problems when it was found. He would have to be careful not to kill again—at least not for a few days. He didn't want to attract too much attention.

Alex stopped at the light in the center of town. Soggy snowflakes were beginning to mix with the cold rain. Looking down the street, Alex saw lights going off in several of the buildings as the stores along Westerberg's main street closed down for the evening. Traffic on the cross street was light. Only a few cars swept past as Alex waited for the light to change. The light turned yellow on the other side, and Alex put the car into gear.

A last car sped through the intersection. It was an old orange Pinto. At the sight of it, Alex was swept by such a wave of memories that he sat through a whole cycle of the light without moving. Image after image skittered across his mind, all of them centered on a smiling girl with copper-red hair. Alex couldn't put a name to the girl, but he knew she was important. Almost as important as feeding.

A car behind him honked, and Alex was startled out of his trance. He turned left and headed down the street after the orange car. He saw the Pinto turn a corner, and pushed his stolen car to catch up. When the orange car went around a second curve, Alex turned off his headlights before closing in. With his night vision, he had no problem seeing the road in the darkness.

The Pinto turned down a small street and pulled into a driveway bordered by a row of tall trees. Alex stopped at the end of the street and waited until the car's lights had gone out. Then he cruised slowly down the street. The house where the car had stopped was an old two-story white house. Seeing it brought more scenes from the past flashing into Alex's head. Again they were images of the red-haired girl.

Alex drove to the end of the block and pulled his car over to the side. He climbed out and walked back toward the house, ignoring the snow that now stuck to his dark suit. On the way he passed another house, one that was dark and empty. But something about it caught Alex's attention. His night vision sensed a strange ruby glow that hung around the house. It smelled of power, and it seemed familiar somehow. Alex shrugged and headed toward the red-haired girl's house.

As usual, being near a house where people lived caused him a strange kind of pain. He pushed through it. He didn't know why, but he had to get near the girl. Lights were on in several parts of the house, but Alex knew where to go. His vision showed him a figure on the second floor—a figure surrounded by a swirl of colors such as Alex had seen in the glow from another person. It had to be the girl.

His fingers gripped the gutter at the corner of the house, and he climbed quickly. There was a ledge around the second floor that was wide enough for him to stand on. He slid along it until he came to a window.

The girl was inside. She was taking off her clothes, getting ready for bed. Alex reached out to touch the window, but a searing pain shot up his arm. He could not get inside the house.

The girl finished undressing and slid into a long nightshirt. She lifted a brush from the nightstand and began to stroke her coppery hair.

Alex leaned as close to the window as he could, so close that pain bit at his nose and cheeks. More memories were coming back. There really had been a time when he didn't live to feed the hunger. And in that time, this girl had been the most important thing in his life.

"Talli," he said softly.

Thirteen

Thursday

Chris pulled the newspaper from the corner vending machine and looked at the first page. As usual, the front of the *Westerberg Leader* didn't say anything important. He put the paper under his arm, let the front of the machine bang closed, and headed for school.

It was winter again in Westerberg. The sky was gray, and the wind was cold, with a hint of more snow to come. Not enough had fallen during the night to stick, but there was a crust of frozen muck on the sidewalk. It crunched under Chris's feet as he walked. The chill wind tugged at the hat he'd decided to keep wearing.

He was glad the moving van had shown up when it was supposed to. There hadn't been time yet to do much but move the boxes into different rooms, but at least Chris had managed to find his heavy winter coat. He hunched his shoulders against a brisk northern wind and wished he'd gotten up early enough to ride in with Donna.

He looked for Talli's car as he passed her house, but the old orange hatchback was already gone. Either they would have to take Talli's car when they went out tonight, or Chris would have to arrange things with Donna.

Chris wasn't sure how he felt about Talli. The thought of getting together with her was both exciting and a little frightening. He supposed it was her looks that had first drawn him to her on the day he came to town, but there was more to her than looks. Ever since he could remember, Chris had loved a mystery. And there was no doubt that Talli was a mystery.

He was so caught up in thoughts of Talli that he walked right into another person standing at the edge of the street.

"Hey, watch out," said the guy.

Chris blinked away tears caused by the cold wind. "Sorry, I guess I was . . ." He stopped and looked more carefully at the figure wrapped in a coat, gloves, and a long red scarf. "Aren't you Paul Katz?"

"Yeah," Katz said. "I told you that myself. You're the guy from Chicago."

"Right. I've been meaning to find you,"

Chris said. "I wanted to ask you some things."

"Sure," Katz replied. "Ask what you want, but let's do it while we're walking, okay? My cousin's car wouldn't start this morning, and I think I'm going to freeze before I get to school."

"Okay. Let's walk."

They crossed the street and headed toward the high school. "So what'd you want to talk about?" asked Katz.

"The people who disappeared," Chris said. "Remember a few days ago? You said the people who were missing were dead."

"No doubt about it," Katz said. "They're gone."

"How do you know?"

Katz stopped and blew out a long breath that steamed in the cold air. "You don't want to know," he said.

"Yeah," Chris said, "I do."

"You think you want to know, but you don't." Katz started walking again. They were almost in the middle of town before he spoke again. "There was this guy named Volker."

"The principal, right?"

Katz looked over at Chris. "You know about Volker?"

"A little. Only what was in the paper."

"Well, I bet they didn't put this in the paper. Volker was a nutcase." He looked at Chris again. His expression made it clear that he didn't expect to be believed. "The very first day

Volker was in town, I got sent to his office."

"What for?"

"For nothing. Volker had people going to the office for breathing wrong. Anyway, there was a girl in there at the same time, Cheryl Fellini."

"Isn't she one of the ones who's missing?" Chris asked.

"Yeah," Katz said with a scowl. "You sure you don't want to tell this yourself?"

"Sorry," Chris said. "I'll try not to interrupt."

"Okay. So I go into the office, and Cheryl is waiting there with Volker. I'm expecting Volker to give us some big lecture about being good. Crap like that. Because you know he's not supposed to touch us." He stopped talking for a second, and Chris would have sworn that Katz was shivering from more than cold. "That isn't how it went," he said.

Katz talked all the way through town and down the hill to school. With his hands stuffed into the pockets of his coat, Chris wasn't able to take any notes, but he didn't need to. If even half of what Katz was telling him was true, then what had happened in Westerberg was far stranger than anything he'd ever read in a mystery novel. If all of it was true, then what had happened was stranger than anything he had imagined.

He didn't interrupt until they were almost at the door of the school. "How much of this did you see?" he asked.

"A lot," Katz said. "After that first trip to Volker's office, I was too sick to go back to school. But I wasn't too sick to look out the window, and I listened to all the things that people said."

"You know someone else I could talk to?" Chris asked.

Katz shrugged. "Maybe, but most of them have changed their stories. Right after it happened, you heard all this weird crap from everybody. By Christmas most of them were pretending it never happened." They stepped up onto the sidewalk in front of the school, and the crunch of ice under their feet turned into the crackle of salt that had been sprinkled on the concrete. "I don't know," said Katz. "Maybe they really believe it didn't happen."

He turned to look at Chris as they stepped inside. His brown eyes picked up a red tinge from the scarf wrapped around his chin, giving him a look that was very disturbing. "They may not remember what happened," Katz said, "but I do." Without another word, he walked off down the hallway.

Chris kicked the ice and salt off his boots and headed for his locker. As he was pulling off his coat, Casey came bounding up with a smile on her face.

"Looking forward to your big date?" she asked.

"Huh? Oh yeah," Chris said. "I guess so."

Casey's eyes widened. "What's wrong with this picture?" she said. "I thought getting a date with Talli was the number-one thing on your top-ten list."

"It is," Chris said. He pulled out his books and slammed the door to his locker. "I'm looking forward to seeing Talli. It's just that I had a long talk with Paul Katz on the way to school."

"Not the Rat again," Casey said. "I thought I told you that he was nuts."

"Well, I guess you may be right. What he told me this morning . . ." Chris shook his head and tried to smile. "Forget it. What are you up to today?"

Casey's grin grew. "About one twenty-two," she said, "but I'm going on a diet."

Chris couldn't help laughing. "You're in a good mood."

"I've got an excuse," she said. "The weather forecast says we'll get a big snow tonight. Maybe we'll get off from school tomorrow."

"Not even one week back after Christmas break, and you're already looking for a day off?" Chris asked, shaking his head.

"Spoken like a true teacher's brother," Casey said. "I take my vacations whenever I can get them." The bell sounded. "Come on," Casey shouted over the noise. "We better hurry."

While the first-period teacher was calling the roll, Chris unfolded his *Westerberg Leader*. He wouldn't have time to read it carefully until later, but there were a few things he could look at right away. He turned a page and ran his finger down a column. Suddenly he stopped. Thirty seconds later he was flipping furiously through the notes he had made.

He looked around the room at all the students laughing and talking in the few minutes left before class began. For everyone's sake, he hoped that Paul Katz was crazy.

"Your play is going to be horror?" Ms. Delany asked.

"I don't mean horror like werewolves and zombies," Talli said. "I want it to be something that will scare people, but make them think at the same time."

Ms. Delany pursed her lips. "Have you thought about the setting?"

Talli nodded. "A small town. We can probably get by with a few walls painted like the inside of houses and some trees and things for outside scenes."

"How many scenes are there?" asked Ms. Delany.

"I don't know that yet," Talli said. "I've just started sketching out the story."

Ms. Delany glanced at her watch. "Come on into the auditorium with me. It's time for the meeting. We can talk more when it's over."

Talli took a seat near the rear of the room

while the rest of the drama club talked about the upcoming production. Another latecomer came in and sat behind her. Most of the others were clustered near the front. They had decided to do a play by an American playwright, and after a bit of discussion, Ms. Delany suggested Thornton Wilder's *Our Town*.

"I had really wanted to do something older," she said, "and *Our Town* has been done a thousand times, but I have to admit that I still cry every time I see it. More important, I think it's a play that the people of this town would like to come and see." She leaned back against the stage. "Let me caution you. This play may look easy, but it's not. No scenery is used. Actors sit out in the audience. *Everything* is on the shoulders of the actors and director." Ms. Delany gave a quick overview of the play, listing the parts that were available, and giving a summary of the story.

"I want the part of the wife," Marcia Malone shouted.

"We'll talk about acting parts in a minute," Ms. Delany said. "We have a more important job to assign first."

"What's more important than the acting?" someone asked.

Ms. Delany walked slowly along the front of the auditorium, and the talking and laughing of the students faded. Talli was amazed at how well the teacher was able to get everyone's attention without saying a word. She thought it would be wonderful if Ms. Delany would take a part in the play herself.

When everything was quiet, Ms. Delany spoke again. "You'll hear a lot of people say that every part in the theater is just as important as any other," she said. "In a way, that's true. Actors can't get along without the prop department. No one will show up unless the publicity people do their job. Without good lighting, it doesn't matter how expressive the actors are. All of that is true."

She stopped in front of the center aisle and her brown eyes swept over the students. "But there's one person who is more important than any other when putting on a play. That person is the director."

"But the teacher who sponsors the club always directs," interjected one boy.

"Not this time," Ms. Delany said. "One of you will be the director. The director has to be both an artist and a capable organizer. The director sets the tone for the play, helps in selecting the cast, helps figure all the costs. In short, the director takes both the responsibility and the blame for everything that happens.

"Now," she concluded, "who would like to be the director for our production of *Our Town?*"

It was so quiet in the theater that Talli could hear the sound of everyone breathing. Just when it seemed that no one was going to volunteer, a slim black guy in the second row stood up. "I'll do it," he said.

Ms. Delany smiled. "Thank you, Mr. Winchell. I'm sure you'll do an excellent job."

Talli was surprised. Grant Winchell was a quiet student, and she couldn't remember his doing anything in the drama club before except the lighting. But she knew he was smart. It was just another example of how Ms. Delany seemed capable of bringing out the best in everyone.

Ms. Delany had Grant come down and sit at the front of the room. They discussed casting for several minutes, then Ms. Delany asked for volunteers for the other behind-the-scenes positions.

"All right," she said at last. "I think we've done all that we can for today. I'll get a copy of the play to our director, and we'll give him a few days to study the script before we have auditions."

"Auditions?" Marcia asked.

"Yes, Ms. Malone. Starting next week, we will have auditions for the major roles in the play." Ms. Delany waved her hands. "Everyone better hurry out of here—we're running pretty late. Remember, we only have six weeks to prepare for this production. I suggest you don't wait until the last minute to get familiar with it. See you all on Monday!"

As the other students were leaving, Talli got

up and walked down to the front of the room where Ms. Delany was still talking with Grant Winchell.

"Don't worry," she was saying. "I'll help out as much as you want. The important thing to remember is that you're in charge. Don't let anyone else, myself included, tell you what to do. Understand?"

"Thanks," Grant said. "I won't let you down."

Ms. Delany's eyes stayed focused on Grant as he walked up the aisle and out of the auditorium. "I think he'll do a fine job," she said to Talli.

"I think so, too," Talli said. "I'm kind of surprised he volunteered."

"So am I. Though I was hoping . . ." Ms. Delany stopped and turned to Talli with a smile. "Weren't we going to talk about your writing?"

"Yes. You were asking me how many scenes there would be."

"Right," Ms. Delany said. "Look, the advice I have for you isn't too different from what I told Grant. This is your play. You have more power over it than even a director—you're creating these people and their lives right out of your mind."

"I guess it's the length of it that scares me most," Talli said. "I've never written anything but a short story before. I'm not sure I can write something as long as a whole play."

"I'm sure you can," Ms. Delany replied. "I read your short story. You did a good job of keeping it small and tight. In a play you can open up a little. Remember that there will be actors up here delivering your lines. You can't *tell* what's inside their heads, as you can in a story, but you can *show* what's in their heads by how you set up the action."

Talli sighed. "It's hard to get started. All that blank paper seems like it's laughing at me."

"This is going to sound like a cliché," said the teacher, "but you can't look at it as a hundred sheets of blank paper. Take it one page at a time. One word at a time."

She bent to pick up her things from a seat in the front row. "Just remember not to stop. The biggest difference between a successful writer and an unsuccessful one is that the successful writer finishes what she starts."

"I'll try," Talli said.

"You'll do more than that," Ms. Delany said. "I'm sure of it."

Fourteen

Alex remembered everything.

It had all come back to him after he climbed down from Talli's window. Standing in the shadow of her house, while snow and sleet pelted down around him, his old life leaked back into his consciousness.

He remembered waiting at the foot of the stairs as Talli came down in a long green dress that she had purchased especially for the junior prom. He remembered crossing the plate to score the winning run and looking up to see her cheering him from the stands. He remembered holding Talli tight. He remembered the feel of her skin under his hand, and the soft pressure of her lips against his.

He could remember everything, every sensation, as clearly as if they had happened only a day before. What he didn't remember was how any of it felt. Sight, and touch, and taste, and smell—all of that was there. But the emotions were gone.

Or almost gone. One thing still burned deep inside Alex from the time before he had given up the day. He still wanted Talli.

He knew where Talli lived. There was nothing to stop him from waiting outside her door. Except that when she saw him, Alex thought, she wouldn't come rushing to hold him. He knew that he had changed. Talli would not want to kiss him, or even touch him, because he was different from her now.

The dream that had come to him the day before had shown him the core of that difference, and the core was Volker. Alex had sat in a chair, and Volker had drained him. He realized now that Volker had been feeding from him, drawing out his energy just as he took the energy of those that he fed from each night. Then Volker had done something else. He had put energy back into Alex. When Alex had gotten out of that chair, he had been different. From that moment on, the hunger had been the center of his life.

Now he had two hungers to feed: the aching need for more energy, and the equally painful need for Talli. If Talli would not accept him for what he was, there was one other way.

Alex would make Talli be like him.

He had fed twice more before the night was out. He swooped down on them as swiftly as a hawk, taking them quickly and completely, and leaving the bodies in a ditch outside of town. He didn't worry about leaving them enough energy to live. Alex thought he would need all the energy he had to get through the next day.

He did not sleep. For the first time since Volker had changed him, he didn't spend any of the day in comfortable darkness. From dawn to dusk, he used his stolen energy to follow Talli.

He was right behind her when she pulled out of her driveway in the morning, and across the street when she parked the car at the school. He waited outside the school for some time; then he decided to go in.

The blue suit he'd been wearing would have been out of place in the school building, but Alex had already thought of that. One of the two victims he had taken during the night had been of high-school age. Alex knew that the guy wouldn't be showing up for school today. As more students trickled into the school, Alex changed his clothes and changed his face. He walked into the school just as the last bell was ringing and stood in the back of the room where Talli sat writing in her notebook.

He sat behind her in two of her morning classes. When Talli went to lunch, Alex was one table away. In an afternoon class he began to feel weak. The windows let in only a little outside light, but it began to burn as the hour wore on. Cautiously, Alex reached his power toward a girl on his right and began to siphon away her energy.

He tried to take only a little, and he stopped when the girl began to look confused and sleepy. It was enough to last Alex only a few minutes. He turned next to the guy on his left, draining enough energy from him to hold out to the end of class.

Alex was relieved to hear the bell ring, signaling the end of the school day. He tried not to be obvious, so he didn't wait for Talli to leave. Instead he hurried to the hall and stood just inside the front door, waiting for her to head outside to her car. Every time one of the exiting students opened the door, pale daylight fell in against Alex's face. With each exposure his skin itched more.

Finally he gave up on waiting and plunged back into the school, forcing his way through the stream of students. He reached the classroom where he had left Talli and peeked inside. Talli was not there. Growling low in his throat, Alex ran down the hall to Talli's locker, but she wasn't there either. He was almost screaming in frustration as he scrambled back to the door. She had gotten away. He knew he shouldn't have let her out of his sight.

Alex flung open the door and raced by several startled students as he headed for his car. He was almost there before he noticed that Talli's car was still in the lot. He leaned against his car. The sunlight felt oven hot, and it was getting hard to think. He squeezed his eyes shut. Talli wasn't in the parking lot, so she must still be inside. He pushed himself away from the car and staggered back toward the school.

It didn't take long to find her. Talli was standing in the hallway, talking with someone Alex recognized as one of Talli's teachers. He hung back as the two talked, then quickly followed as they went into the auditorium.

The auditorium was wonderfully dim, and Alex felt better as soon as he stepped into it. He took a seat right behind Talli. He reached out very carefully and touched her red hair so gently that she did not turn. Her hair felt electric under his fingers. For a moment Alex was overwhelmed with the urge to feed from her, but he shoved the impulse down.

Following Talli all day was getting him nowhere. Alex already knew what he had to do. He had to make Talli over so that she, too, would know the hunger. Then they would be together through night after endless night.

When the other students got up to leave, Alex went with them to the top of the aisle, but he didn't leave the auditorium. Instead he moved into the corner, watching from the shadows as Talli spoke again to the young teacher with the dark hair.

The two of them seemed close, Alex noticed. The teacher smiled at Talli and Talli smiled back. It stirred up other feelings in Alex, feelings that he couldn't quite put a name to.

He wanted Talli all to himself. That meant

changing her. Alex knew how it had been done to him, or at least he thought he did. But suppose he didn't do things right. Could he make someone else be like him, or had only Volker had that power? He would have to test it. If he drained all the energy from Talli and wasn't able to put it back, then she would simply be dead. That wasn't what he wanted at all.

He had to experiment. Then, when he was sure he knew how to make the trick work properly, he would work it on Talli. In the meantime he would keep an eye on her. But there was no reason to follow her every minute. Talli had lived in Westerberg all her life. She wasn't going anywhere.

If he could see her every day and know that she was still here, things would be fine. He just needed the proper role to play, a way to stay close without being obvious.

Talli and the teacher finished their talk. Talli gathered her things and headed up the aisle. Alex watched her go, but he didn't follow her. Instead he stayed hidden in the corner, watching the young teacher as she picked up her things. He let the contours of his face and body slip back into his natural form. There was no reason to hide his face now.

When the teacher started to leave the auditorium, Alex stepped out of the shadows. She stopped, startled. "Can I help you?" she asked.

"Yes," said Alex. "I think you can." He smiled as he walked down the aisle toward her.

Fifteen

By the time they reached the diner, the sun was sitting low in the hills to the west. Talli steered the car into an open slot in front of the wide glass window.

"I hope this is okay," she said.

"Sure," said Chris. "It looks fine."

Talli turned off the car. She started to get out, then looked over at Chris with a strange expression.

"What is it?" he asked.

She shook her head. "I don't know. I guess it's been a long time since I had someone else riding in my car."

A few flakes of snow were starting to fall as they went into the diner, but the darkening sky still showed patches of deep blue. The predicted snowstorm hadn't shown up yet. Talli paused inside the door to take off her coat. "I can't stay too late," she said. "School tomorrow and everything."

"That's fine," Chris replied. "I should probably be studying myself." He took her coat from her and hung it on the rack near the door, then followed it with his own coat and the damp fedora. "Where do you want to sit?" he asked, running his fingers through his hat-smashed hair.

"Let's get a booth," Talli said. "I always like the booths." She led the way past a long white Formica counter and rows of shiny tables to a booth upholstered in faded green vinyl.

Talli picked up a menu. "This probably seems like a real hick place to you," she said.

"Nope," Chris said. "We have places that look a whole lot like this back in Chicago. I've always liked diners. You can get something to eat without standing in line, and you don't have to worry about how you're dressed."

Talli smiled. "That's what I like about this place, too." She put down the menu and looked out the window. "This diner's been here for years. It used to be really busy, but these days it seems like everybody goes to the fast-food places down along the new highway."

"I never got into fast-food places," Chris replied. He picked up his own menu and browsed through the selections. A waitress in a uniform that looked as old as the diner came over and took their order. After she was gone, there was a long silence. Chris thought of asking about the disappearances, or telling Talli about his suspicions, but he didn't. It was just too soon.

"My sister says you're a writer," he said at last.

"Not really," Talli said with a shake of her head. "I wrote some stories once, and I guess they were okay. Mostly I'm a reader."

"Me, too," Chris said. "I mean, I'm a reader, too. Mysteries are what I like best. Everything from Agatha Christie to hard-boiled detectives. I like them all."

"I've read some mysteries, but what I read is mostly horror." She stopped and glanced again at the window. "Or at least, I used to."

"Used to?"

Talli shrugged. "I haven't read much lately."

"Since November?" Chris asked.

Talli looked back at him in silence.

"I'm sorry," he said. "I really didn't mean to bring it up tonight. Especially with this being our first time alone together."

"That's okay," Talli replied. "I can't say I wasn't thinking about it anyway."

"I guess it's on everyone's minds," Chris said. "Ever since I got to Westerberg, people have been talking about it, and I can't help thinking about it myself."

They both grew quiet as the waitress came back to the table and starting setting down plates of food. For a few minutes after she left, they busied themselves with moving forks and knives and sampling their food.

"Casey said you were checking on things at the library," Talli said between bites of roast beef.

"Yeah. I'm sorry," he said. "I didn't want to hurt anyone."

Talli shook her head vigorously. "No, I'm not upset about your looking," she said. "I wish someone would have looked sooner. I tried to get people to pay attention to what was going on back when it happened. If they had, then maybe . . . maybe . . . well, you know."

"Maybe everyone wouldn't be gone," Chris finished for her.

She nodded quickly. "Have you found out anything?"

"I know that one of the missing principals, Mr. Volker, was involved in it," he said. "Everything started happening when he came to town, and everything stopped after he disappeared. I don't think that was simply coincidence."

Talli opened her mouth as if she were going to say something, but closed it again. "What I don't know is what he was up to," Chris continued. "Everybody talks about drugs, but no matter how I look at the problem, drugs don't seem to fit."

"No," Talli said softly. "I guess they don't."

"I can see how drugs might fit in with the

missing students. Maybe they got too close to Volker's operations." Chris stopped and frowned. "What I can't figure out is how Volker relates to the deaths."

Talli stopped eating and looked at Chris with a strange expression. "Deaths? What do you mean, deaths?"

"All the deaths in town that occurred that week," explained Chris. He put down his fork, reached into his pocket, and pulled out a folded sheet of paper. "See?" he said as he smoothed out the sheet on the table. "The week before Volker showed up, there were six deaths in the area. Volker shows up, and there are fourteen. Then the next week, after Volker is gone, it goes right back to five."

"Fourteen deaths," Talli said. She leaned over the sheet of paper and looked at the list of names Chris had written. "None of these are the missing students," she said.

"That's right."

"These are more deaths. I didn't even know about these."

"More deaths?" Chris asked. He reached across the table and took Talli's hand. "Talli, are the missing students dead?"

Talli shivered, but she didn't pull away. She closed her eyes for a moment, then nodded. "As far as I know," she said, "they're all dead."

"Was it Volker?"

"Yes," Talli said. "It was Volker." She

squeezed Chris's hand for a moment, then pulled her fingers free. Talli's green eyes fixed on Chris. "Do you . . . do you want to hear the rest?" she asked in a small voice.

Chris nodded. "If you want to tell me," he said.

Talli took a deep breath and stared down at the table. "Volker," she said, "was a monster."

"That's what Paul Katz said," Chris told her.

"Katz? What does he know?"

"He says he saw Volker do something to some of the other students. Something that made them pass out or die. And he says he saw Volker taking people—students—in and out of his house." Chris rubbed at his chin and shook his head. "I don't know if I believe everything he told me, but if you listen to him, Volker was some kind of vampire."

"He *was* a vampire," Talli said. "But not the kind you see in movies." Her eyes were focused on nothing, and her face was tight. "I don't think he drank blood. It was more like he pulled the life right out of people. Sometimes it happened quickly. Sometimes it didn't." Her eyes moved back to Chris. "You're living in Samantha Deveraux's house, aren't you?"

He nodded. "Donna bought the house from Samantha's parents."

"I saw Samantha die. It wasn't fast, and it wasn't easy. It took her about three days to go from being seventeen to looking like she was old enough to be her own great-great-grandmother." Talli shivered so violently that the plates on the table rattled. "I saw her turn to dust," she whispered.

Chris swallowed hard. "Is that what happened to all of them?" he asked.

"No, I think most of the others . . ." She stopped and blinked. "You think I'm crazy, don't you?"

"No," he said. "I probably *should* think you're crazy, but I don't. Katz thinks you were involved in the deaths. He thinks you had something to do with Volker."

"In a way, he's right," Talli said, leaning back in the booth. "I guess I never expected to tell this story to anyone, and I certainly never thought Katz the Rat would figure it out." She leaned forward again and gripped the edge of the table with her tense fingers. "We could probably spend all night talking about it, but 'vampire' is the best word I can find to describe Volker. I think he killed most of them. I think he drained the life right out of them and threw them away. But some of them he made into things like himself. He had a bunch of them hidden under the cover of a closed swimming pool in back of the house he was renting."

"What happened to them?" asked Chris. "The ones in the pool, I mean."

"I killed them," Talli said. "If 'killed' is the right word. I pulled the cover off the pool and the sunlight burned them to ashes."

Chris stared at her, hardly able to breathe. "You killed them?" he whispered.

Talli shrugged. "I don't even know if they were still alive. Vampires in books are supposed to be dead—maybe they were already dead, too. They certainly weren't *human*. I didn't mean to burn them up; I was just trying to get away."

"Wow," Chris said without thinking.

"Now you *really* think I'm crazy, don't you?" Talli said.

"No, I don't," he said, shaking his head. "It's just that I've been trying to figure out what happened to those missing people all week. Heck, the whole town is sitting here wondering where those people disappeared to. And now you tell me that you've known all along."

"What was I supposed to do?" asked Talli. "Go to the police? Can you imagine what they would have said if I told them that all the missing kids turned into vampires and I killed them?"

"They would have locked you up and thrown away the key," Chris said.

"Right. My dad's a police officer. I tried a couple of times to tell him about what had really happened." She sighed and pushed her red hair away from her face. "That's how I ended up having so many *wonderful* interviews with the school counselor."

Chris glanced down at the rumpled piece of

paper on the table. "Were there others? You said Volker had some of the ones that he changed in the pool. Were there some in other places?"

"Morris South," Talli said.

"Casey said something about him. She didn't like him very much."

"I didn't even know him before Volker came," Talli said. "He acted crazy after he met Volker, maybe he was crazy before."

"You folks about done?" asked a voice.

Startled, Chris looked up to see the waitress standing over them. "Not quite," he said. "We'll be a bit longer."

"Well, we're closing in ten minutes. If you're going to want any pie or anything, you best order it now."

Chris glanced down and saw that the food on his and Talli's plates had barely been touched. "I don't think I'll be wanting anything," he said.

"Me neither," Talli added. "Thanks."

"I'll go get your check," said the waitress.

"I didn't realize we'd been talking so long," Talli said.

Chris smiled. "I wanted to hear it, and I think that you needed to tell it."

They took time to eat a few bites before the waitress came back. Chris grabbed the check from her. "Let me pay this," he said.

Talli's green eyes narrowed. "I didn't know Chicago was still in the Stone Age," she said. "Women can pull their own weight."

"You drove, I feed. It works out," Chris said.

"All right," Talli said. "I guess I'll let it slide this time."

They collected their things and went outside. It had grown completely dark while they talked, and large flakes of snow were drifting slowly down from an absolutely still black sky. Talli's car made dark tracks in the fresh white blanket as they left the parking lot and started for home.

"My parents would usually be mad at me for staying out this late on a school night," Talli said. "But they were so glad to hear I was going out with someone, they'll probably let me off easy."

"One advantage to major trauma, I guess," Chris said.

Talli glanced at him in confusion, then laughed. "I don't think I'll try it again, just the same." She turned on the windshield wipers as the snow started to stick. "It'll be a pretty snow if it stays like this," she said. "With no wind, it'll cover everything."

"You think we'll have school tomorrow?" Chris asked.

"I don't know. If it's not really bad, we probably will. We missed a lot of school back before Christmas."

"If we do," he said, "you want to get together?"

Talli was quiet for a moment. "I don't know,"

she said finally. "I like you, Chris, but I need some time to think."

They drove several blocks in silence. "It's a shame I don't know where Volker is," Chris said at last. "He should have to answer for all those deaths."

"He already did," Talli said.

"What do you mean?"

Talli brought the car to a stop and twisted in her seat to face him. "I killed Volker, too."

Chris sat frozen in astonishment. It was hard to believe that someone as small and pretty as Talli had taken out a whole vampire army. But then, his sister Donna was no bigger, and she had taken on the whole world. "You're very impressive," he said.

"I had to do it," Talli said. "He was killing everyone. I had to stop him."

Chris reached over and put his hand on her shoulder. "I'm sure you did what you had to," he said. "It's amazing that you managed to stop him when so many others couldn't."

They drove on to Talli's house. "You can stop here," Chris said. "It'll only take me two minutes to walk to my house."

He was surprised when Talli leaned over and kissed him. She pulled away before he could respond. "Thanks, Chris," she said. "I did need to talk about it."

Chris climbed out of the car. He was about to say good night when he remembered something else. He opened the door and climbed back into the Pinto.

"What is it?" Talli asked. "Something wrong?"

"There's one thing I didn't tell you," he said. "You remember I said that there were six deaths in the county the week before Volker came, and five the week after?"

"Yeah. What about it?"

Chris took a deep breath. "I checked every week from then till now, and most of the weeks last year. There was one week with nine deaths, but that was only because of a big car accident. Besides that one, no week had more than seven deaths."

"So?"

"So this week there were eleven," he said.

Talli stared at Chris in stunned silence. "You think there's another one?" she asked after several seconds. Chris could hear the panic in her voice. "Another one like Volker?"

"You said he made others like himself," Chris said. He reached across in the darkness and found Talli's hands. "Talli, are you sure you got them all?"

Sixteen

Marcia Malone had opened her car door and was starting to slide inside when Alex approached her. She turned at the sound of footsteps on the blacktop. Alex stopped about five feet from her. The lighted window of the hamburger place was behind him, and he watched her squint against the glare.

"Hi, Marcia," he said.

She put a hand over her eyes, trying to block out the light. "Hi," she said uncertainly.

Alex stepped forward. The light showed the curve of his face and gleamed from his wavy brown hair. "I thought maybe you'd like to go somewhere."

"Alex?" Marcia gasped. "Alex Cole?"

"That's right, Marcia," Alex said. "What about it? You want to go somewhere? Maybe get something to eat?"

Still squinting, Marcia took a step toward him. "Alex! I thought you were gone. I mean, *everybody* thought you were gone."

Alex smiled. "I was gone, but I came back. Come on, let's go somewhere and I'll tell you all about it."

Marcia frowned. "I don't know, Alex. Does anyone know you're here? Where are the rest of them? Where's my brother?"

"The rest of them," Alex repeated. He leaned against a car and pushed his hands into the pockets of his jeans. "Truth is, Marcia, I don't know where your brother or any of the rest of them are right now. I've been on my own all this time."

"Really?" Marcia asked. "I guess we all thought you and Lisa ran off with the others."

"No. Just me." Alex straightened and glanced around at the restaurant as a group of people came out and headed for their cars. "Come on, Marcia," he said. "Let's go somewhere else. This isn't a good place to talk. Let's go eat and we can talk about your brother." He stepped closer.

Marcia backed away. "Maybe we can talk tomorrow," she said. "Besides, I've already eaten. I'm not hungry anymore."

"I'm still hungry, Marcia," Alex said. "Very, very hungry."

Marcia yanked her car door open and jumped inside, but Alex was too fast for her. He had her out of the car and halfway across the parking lot before she could stop him. She tried to scream, but he clamped his hand across her mouth and the sound was nothing but a faint moan.

By the time they reached the van Alex had taken from his first victim of the night, Marcia was unconscious. Alex tossed her into the back, next to the body that was already lying there, and headed out of the parking lot. The laughing people at the fast-food restaurant never even glanced at the dark van as he drove past them.

Alex fed wherever he found a likely victim, but for what he was going to do tonight, he needed a private place to work. He drove through the town with Marcia bouncing in the back of the van. As he passed Talli's house, he slowed down, but the window of her room was dark. Alex went two doors down and pulled over to the side. He killed the headlights and hopped out of the van.

The house was taller than the others in the neighborhood. Its walls had once been a pure white, but now they showed the cracking and peeling of neglect. The long windows were dark and vacant. Along one side of the house the gutter had torn loose and dangled to the ground, giving the house a twisted, broken look. It had been Volker's house. Once Talli had brought Alex to this place to try to find her friend Lisa. Now it was empty and silent. It was the perfect place for Alex.

There was a heavy chain across the gate to the house. Alex took the chain in his hands and pulled. Slowly the metal links stretched until they suddenly parted with a loud snap. Alex dropped the chain to the cold street and pushed open the iron gate. He got back into the van and drove through.

Leaving the other body in the van, he carried Marcia Malone through the darkened driveway and up the stone steps to the front of the house. He held her with one hand while his night vision scanned the house. As he had expected, there was no one there. But a strange red-green glow lingered over the house. Alex could feel the power when he touched his hand to the brass plate on the front door. Volker had left something of himself here. Alex hoped it would help guide him in what he had to do.

A single blow from his hand was enough to snap the lock and send the front door swinging in to darkness. He pulled Marcia inside and closed the door. He had been in the house only once before, with Talli. Following his memory of that visit, Alex lifted Marcia in his arms and carried her up the wide curving staircase to the second floor.

There were doors down both sides of the hallway. He went past the first few doors, before shoving open one on the right. His memory was good—it was the room he was looking for. Most of Volker's house had been unfurnished, but this one room held a bed and dresser. The last time Alex had seen this room, the rapidly aging Samantha Deveraux had been here. Alex wondered briefly what had happened to her.

He walked over to the bed and put Marcia on top of the colorful blankets. Coarse ashes crunched under his feet as he walked. The window in this room was the only one that had been covered with drapes. Now the drapes lay in a heap below the window. The window itself had been broken, and the room left open to the weather. Alex could see where the carpet under the window had been faded by rain and sun. Nearby was a black-and-brown place where it looked as if something had been burned. Things had happened in this room that he did not understand. He didn't let it worry him.

The clouds parted for a moment, and silvery moonlight poured through the shattered window. Marcia groaned. Alex turned around in time to see her eyes flicker open. As soon as she saw him, she gasped. Her hands clawed at the bed as she tried to push away from him. He stepped across the dirty carpet and caught her by one ankle. With a sharp pull he brought her sliding back across the bed.

Her breath was coming in fast sobs. "You killed them," she said in a hoarse whisper. "That's where they all went. You killed them."

Alex shook his head. "I didn't kill them," he

said. “I already told you that I don’t know what happened to them.”

Marcia sniffed. “Really?”

“Really.”

She turned her head, looking around the room in the dim moonlight. “Where are we?” she asked.

“In a house.”

“Whose house?”

“Mine now,” Alex said. He let go of Marcia’s ankles and moved closer to her head.

She started to sit up. “How did we get here?” she asked. Alex didn’t answer. “I guess it doesn’t matter,” she said quickly. “Can we leave? I’d really like to go home.” The terror in her eyes had faded when Alex said he hadn’t killed the others, but fear was coming back into her face now. Her voice trembled, and the pale moonlight sparkled in the tears that were forming in her eyes.

“Please?” she asked.

“We’ll go very soon,” Alex said. He sat down on the edge of the bed at her side. He held out his left hand. Marcia hesitated for a moment, then took it. He smiled at her. Then he reached up with his right hand and shoved her back against the bed. A scream boiled up out of her throat, but Alex was already drawing in her energy. The scream turned into a strangled whisper, then a sigh, then nothing.

He drained her slowly. The hunger sparked

at the back of his mind, demanding that he pull the life from her more quickly. Alex resisted, letting the energy come into him slowly. Just a trickle. The glow around her body faded from sun yellow, to dull amber, to a faint brown. Then the glow was gone. Marcia was dead.

Alex closed his eyes. He knew what he had to do, but it was like trying to move muscles that had never worked before. Long seconds passed while Alex strained to open the tap and let the energy flow backward. At last he found the switch in his mind. The energy burst out in a torrent of green and scarlet. Marcia's body jerked and twitched as the flood roared over her. Pain swept through Alex. He threw his head back and howled in agony. It took all the strength he had left to slam the gate closed and keep what little energy remained from spilling out.

Alex fell to the carpet, his night vision dim and his head ringing with pain. It took him several minutes to gather enough energy to stand up and brush the ashes from his shirt. He staggered over to the bed and peered down at Marcia.

She wasn't moving, but a glow had again surrounded her form. It didn't look the way Alex had expected it to. Whenever he looked down at himself with his night vision, he saw a green light. The light was dim now, but still there. Around the form of Marcia, the glow was filled with threads of red. As Alex watched, the green faded and the red threads merged and darkened. Her whole form became covered in a shroud of light that was as dark and red as a pool of blood. She did not move.

Alex growled and looked out the window. His first experiment had been a failure, but it was still early in the evening. There might still be time to feed and try again with someone else.

The bedsprings squeaked, and Alex turned quickly. Marcia was sitting up in the bed. Her eyes were still closed, but they moved behind the lids as if she were dreaming. Her fingers tightened on the bed, pulling at the blankets.

Alex smiled. It had not been for nothing, after all. He had worked the miracle.

He reached out and put his hand on Marcia's shoulder. "Are you awake?" he asked.

Her mouth fell open, and she let out a scream that made the walls vibrate. With a twist of her arm she struck Alex a backhanded blow that sent him flying across the room. He hit the wall so hard that plaster dust rained down from the ceiling. He rolled over and raised his arms, ready to block another blow.

Marcia was still on the bed. Her mouth opened and closed, but no more sound came out. Her eyelids sprang open, but the eyes they revealed were balls of red fire. Her body jerked and tossed, bouncing up and down so violently that the bed rattled like a passing train.

Alex stood up. He remembered being weak and in pain after Volker had changed him, but he didn't remember anything like this. He stepped toward her, but stayed out of reach of her thrashing arms. Her first blow had been very strong, and while it hadn't hurt Alex, it had taken much of his small supply of remaining energy. "Marcia?" he called. "Can you hear me?"

Her face turned toward him and the glowing red eyes seemed to brighten. Alex would have thought himself beyond surprise, and certainly incapable of fear. But a second later he rediscovered both these things.

Like a puppet being drawn up on strings, Marcia rose from the bed and hung suspended in the air. Her mouth opened again, and she hissed like a basket of cobras. Then she fell on him.

Her fingers tightened on him like claws, and her teeth clamped down on his shoulder. Alex bellowed and tried to throw her off, but he was too weak. All of a sudden Marcia stopped biting at him and drew back. Alex watched from inches away as her face changed. The cheeks became hollow and thin. Her flaming eyes narrowed to slits. Her mouth widened until it reached almost from ear to ear. When it opened again, the teeth inside were like curving daggers.

Alex strained against the thing that he had made. The reshaped head darted forward and the sharp teeth tore a hunk of flesh from Alex's shoulder. Green fire spilled out, lighting the room with its glow. The monster that had been a girl drew back, and Alex kicked at it, forcing it away with his legs.

The thing stood up and hissed down at Alex. Its legs had changed shape, becoming twisted and bent at an impossible angle. Its arms grew short. At the same time, its fingers stretched out into claws a foot long. They dangled from the twisted hands and rattled together like bits of bone. The monster's neck grew longer. The head, which had become lumpy and misshapen, dangled down from bulging shoulders. It screamed and took an awkward step forward.

Alex scrambled back in horror. The wound on his shoulder was still leaking energy, and he felt sure that another attack would be more than he could take.

The creature stopped. Its flesh began to flow and move as if it were filled with worms. The short arms beat at the air. The head bobbed and swayed on the end of the long neck as the features of the face flowed and changed like wax near a fire.

Suddenly the mangled face re-formed into that of Marcia Malone. "Help me," she cried. "Please help me."

Then red fire poured out of the boiling eyes. The monster fell backward, seeming to shrink as it fell. In seconds there was nothing left but a pile of smoldering ash.

Alex stood up, holding one hand to his

wounded shoulder. This was not the way. Whatever Volker had done to make him, Alex had not remembered correctly. If he had done this to Talli, she would be dead.

Now he had to get out of the house and feed. If he was going to follow the plan he had made for the coming day, he would need all the energy he could get. He looked down at the pile of ash and scowled. This had been a mistake.

But he would do better next time.

Seventeen

Friday

Chris wasn't sure if he should be excited or worried. On the one hand, he had finally gotten to be alone with Talli, and he had learned what was behind the mystery that had been bothering him ever since he reached town. On the other hand, it had been a lot easier to believe Talli when they were sitting in a booth in the corner of a dark café.

With the cold light of morning pouring through the kitchen window and a bowl of cornflakes staring him in the face, it was hard to believe in vampires. But if what Talli had said wasn't true, that meant that Talli really was crazy. Chris didn't want to believe that. If what she had said was true, then the extra deaths in the paper might mean that there was another vampire in the area. He didn't want to believe that either.

Chris put his hands to his head and squeezed. It was awfully early in the morning for a headache.

When everything was weighed, Chris decided it was easier just to believe in the vampire. Maybe that meant that he was crazy, but he thought it would be a bad idea to say there were no such things as vampires if there really were. Better safe than sorry. After all, even Katz the Rat had said Volker was a vampire—two people couldn't possibly come up with the exact same crazy story. Besides, if he believed in the monster, that meant he could believe in Talli. Chris really wanted to believe in Talli.

As he got up to refill his cereal bowl, Chris noticed that it was after seven. He hadn't even seen Donna come down the stairs yet. He glanced out the window and saw that her car was still in the driveway. The light dusting of snow that had fallen overnight was undisturbed.

"Donna!" he shouted up the stairs. "You up?"

There was no reply. Chris thought back to the night before. Donna usually went to bed early, so he hadn't seen her at all after he got home from his dinner with Talli. Suddenly worried, Chris put down his bowl and trotted up the stairs to Donna's room.

He rapped his knuckles against the door. "Donna? You up?"

"Yes," she said.

"You decent?"

"Yes."

Chris pushed the door open and looked inside. Donna was standing in front of her dresser. "You okay?" he asked.

"Sure," Donna said without turning. She reached up and ran a hand across her dark hair.

"You sound bad," Chris said. "You got a cold starting?"

"Yeah, maybe." She leaned over and picked up a brush from the table, taking a few swipes at her hair.

"That what you're wearing to school today?" he asked.

She turned halfway around and looked at him. "Something wrong with what I'm wearing?" Donna had on a sweater and dark jeans, instead of the more formal clothes she usually wore for teaching.

Chris shrugged. "It looks fine. It's just not your usual little-old-teacher ensemble."

Donna glanced in the mirror again and put down her brush. "I was . . . afraid it might snow today," she said. "I wanted to wear something warm."

"Good idea. The radio still says there's a big one on the way." Chris glanced at his watch. "I guess I'll go back downstairs and finish my breakfast. Aren't you supposed to be there by now?"

Donna turned to the clock on the bed stand. "It's only seven fifteen," she said.

"Yeah, but I thought you had to be there early."

She looked at Chris for a moment. "You're right," she said. She shook her head and smiled weakly. "This cold must be bothering me more than I thought."

Chris headed back downstairs, with Donna close behind. He sat down at the table and poured milk onto a second helping of cornflakes as his sister struggled into her heavy coat.

"What time are you getting home tonight?" Donna asked.

"I don't have anything planned," Chris said. "Unless I do something with Talli."

Donna stopped with her coat still dangling from one arm. "Talli . . . McAlister," she said.

"Sure. You're the one that said you thought we'd be good for each other," Chris said. Donna just stared at him. Chris looked at her more closely. "You sure you feel like going in today?" he asked. "You look completely out of it."

"Yes," she said. "I'll be fine." She shoved her arm into the empty sleeve and pulled the coat tight. "Do you want to ride in with me?"

"No," Chris said. "Casey offered to give me a ride, and I already told her to stop for me."

"Casey. Right." Donna walked across the

kitchen and picked up her car keys from the counter. "I better get going, then."

Chris laughed. "Hey, there's one benefit of your cold."

Donna stopped in the door and turned to him with a puzzled frown. "What's that?"

"You found your car keys by yourself," Chris said, still grinning.

His sister blinked at him. "So?"

Chris's smile died. "Never mind."

Donna picked up her briefcase and walked out to the car. Chris stood and went to the window to watch her drive down the street. He should have checked to see if she was running a fever. Not that it would have done much good. Donna had always hated to miss school, even when she was a student. Now that she was a teacher, she'd probably have gone in with two broken legs and a case of bubonic plague. Chris bit his lip and hoped she'd be okay.

Ten minutes later Casey pulled into the driveway and leaned on the horn of her small red pickup. Chris hurried to grab his things and run outside.

"Cold enough for you, Chicago?" Casey asked as he climbed into the truck.

"More than cold enough," Chris replied. He leaned against the window and looked up at the iron-gray sky. "When's that snowstorm coming?"

Casey shifted the truck through its gears. "I don't know. It was supposed to be here already.

Maybe we'll get out of school early."

"That would be nice," Chris said. "I've spent so much time checking into these disappearances, I don't have a clue what's going on in most of my classes. I could use an afternoon to catch up."

"That's the problem with being a great detective while you're still in high school," Casey said. "So how did your date with Talli go?"

"It wasn't really a date. We just went to the diner and talked."

"You went out alone, you ate dinner together, and you talked." Casey shook her head. "I don't know. It sure sounds like a date to me."

Chris laughed. "All right. It was a date."

"So? Are you going to tell me about it, or do I have to hurt you?"

"It was . . . interesting," Chris said.

"Interesting?" Casey repeated. "Uh-oh. That doesn't sound like a dream date. You guys must not have hit it off as well as I thought you would."

"We hit it off fine," said Chris. "It's just that we talked about some strange things. It wasn't exactly the most light and cheerful dinner in the world."

Casey glanced over at him. "You asked Talli about the missing students, didn't you?"

"Well, I didn't exactly *ask* her. . . ."

"What am I going to do with you, Delany?" Casey said in mock disgust. "Do I have to give you lessons in polite conversation? I suppose you told her all about your research in the local paper, too."

Chris held up his hands. "I confess. I'm guilty. But I think she wanted to talk about it. No, I think she's been *dying* to talk about it, and she was afraid no one would listen to her."

"So it was a good date," Casey said.

"Yeah," Chris replied. "I guess it was a good date. Only . . ." He stopped and shrugged. "I guess talking about those things left me feeling kind of scared."

Casey reached across the seat and patted his arm. "Don't worry, Delany. Next time I'll give you some cue cards so you'll know the right things to say."

Chris couldn't hold back a grin. "Gee," he said. "Would you?"

"What are friends for?"

Talli pulled open her curtains and looked out at the day. The sky was heavily overcast, and she could almost feel the weight of the snow pressing down. It looked an awful lot as it had in November when all the trouble had happened. There had been snow then, too. She let the curtains fall over the glass and went to get dressed.

Talli could hardly believe all the things she had said to Chris the night before. They had met only a few days ago, and she was spilling things to him that she would never have told any of her remaining friends. Despite what he had said, Talli was sure that Chris thought she was an absolute nut.

She waited for one of the voices in her head to comment, but they had been quiet for days. Working on the play had helped, and talking to Chris had helped even more. It was strange that she was worried about his thinking she was crazy, because for the first time in weeks Talli was sure that she was sane.

She dressed quickly and turned to the stack of papers on her desk. After coming in from her dinner with Chris, Talli had felt full of energy. Ideas about her play seemed to be coming to her faster than she could write them, and she had stayed up late into the night working those ideas into a solid form. By the time she stopped, there were over twenty scribbled pages on the table.

It had been almost midnight, but Talli would have kept working if it hadn't been for the howling. Somewhere nearby, some poor animal had let out a moan that sounded so tortured, it had made Talli put down her pen and look out the window. She didn't see an animal, but for a moment she thought she had seen a light coming from the upper floor of Volker's empty house. It was gone in a blink, and Talli had put it down to being tired. After that she hadn't felt much like writing and had gone to bed.

Talli gathered all the pages and shoved them in a folder as she headed out the door. She was both anxious and nervous about showing the pages to Ms. Delany. She wanted the teacher's approval, but she was afraid Ms. Delany might think her play was really strange.

Only a very small amount of snow had fallen through the night, and Talli didn't bother to dust it off before she started her car. She just coasted back down the driveway, then let the wind blow the snow away in white streamers as she sped down the road. When she reached the stoplight in the center of town, Casey Pays's red truck was two cars ahead of Talli. She could see the silhouette of someone riding in the passenger seat, and she knew right away it was Chris.

Talli was tempted to honk or wave, but she held back. She didn't want to talk to Chris until she had worked out what to say. She only hoped that Chris and Casey weren't up there making fun of what she had told him at the diner.

It wasn't until she was sitting through her first class that Talli really started thinking about what Chris had told her. If he was right, then there was another vampire in town. Talli could feel panic building inside her at the thought.

If there was a new vampire, it could be someone that Talli didn't know, or it could be one of the victims of Volker. While Talli had destroyed many of Volker's young vampires, she had no idea if she had gotten them all. Morris South had been able to get out and work for Volker.

Maybe there had been others like him that Talli didn't know about.

She tried to go through the list of missing people in her mind, eliminating those she knew were dead. It didn't work—there were too many faces that Talli wasn't able to cross off. If there really was a vampire . . .

It could be anyone, said one of her internal voices.

The pencil she was writing with snapped in her hand, making a noise like a firecracker. People for several desks on each side turned to look at Talli, and there were a few snickers. She put the broken pencil in her bag, pulled out another, and pretended to go on with her notes.

Talli tried not to think about Chris's vampire as she went through the rest of the morning. Instead she concentrated on rewriting and expanding the notes she had made on her play. She stayed tense for hours, expecting the voices to come back, but except for the one outburst, they were quiet.

By the time Ms. Delany's class rolled around after lunch, Talli was very excited. Her midnight scribbling read much better than she had expected. It wasn't a play, but it seemed to Talli that she had made a solid core of story to build a play around. She spent the last minutes before the start of class recopying the story neatly so she could give it to Ms. Delany.

When she got to the classroom, most of the

other students were gathered at the window. The gray clouds had finally opened up, and heavy snow was falling so thickly that the cars on the far end of the parking lot were invisible behind the blowing sheets of white.

Talli was surprised to see Ms. Delany dressed casually in jeans and a sweater. Class was very different, too. Instead of her usual exciting lesson, Ms. Delany said she wasn't feeling well and asked the students to read from their books. Her hoarse voice certainly sounded as if she were coming down with a cold. Talli was disappointed, but decided to spend the time making a few last-minute changes to her play idea before she turned it in.

Ten minutes into class, the announcement that everyone had been expecting came. "Attention," said the crackly voice over the intercom. "Because of the snowfall, classes will be suspended for the afternoon."

The cheer in the class was so loud, it was almost impossible to hear the rest of the announcement. Before the class had quieted, the bell sounded. The rest of the students grabbed for their things and almost ran for the door.

Talli glanced up to see that Ms. Delany was already looking at her. Swallowing her nervousness, Talli picked up her papers and headed for the teacher's desk.

"Hello, Talli," Ms. Delany said.

"Hi." Talli held out her idea. "I thought you

might want to look at this before I went any further."

Ms. Delany didn't even glance at the papers before putting them on her desk. "I'll get to those later," she said. "First, I'd like to talk to you about something."

Talli was puzzled, but she nodded. "Okay."

The teacher waited until the other students had left the room before continuing. "I understand that you've been dating my brother," she said.

"We're not really dating, Ms. Delany," Talli said. She was surprised that Ms. Delany would bring this up at school, and she felt a bit of a blush creeping into her face. "We just had dinner together."

Ms. Delany smiled. "It's all right, Talli. I'm not mad."

Talli was confused. Why would Ms. Delany be mad? It made no sense. "Um, good," Talli said slowly.

"I thought you might want to come by our house tonight," said the teacher. "It's very close to your house, so you wouldn't have to drive in the snow. Come over and have dinner with us."

Again Talli was surprised. She was glad that Ms. Delany had invited her, but it felt strange to have a teacher ask her to come over. "Okay," she said. "Should I bring anything?"

"Just bring yourself," Ms. Delany said. "That'll be enough."

Talli smiled uncertainly and left the room. She went to her locker and shoved her books inside. Though she had spent most of the week working on her play instead of doing her homework, she wasn't in a mood to take things home and study. As she was leaving the school, she ran into Chris waiting at the doorway.

"Hi," he said. "I don't suppose I can bum a ride, can I?"

"Sure," Talli said.

"Thanks," Chris replied. "I was supposed to ride back with Casey, but I haven't seen her since we got to school this morning."

Eighteen

Casey Pays fought hard.

Alex thought she was still unconscious when he took her from the janitor's closet where he had left her during morning classes. He waited until the halls were empty of students and teachers before he opened the door. Casey was still lying as he left her, crumpled in the middle of the dust mops and cans of sawdust.

But as he was dragging her to the car, she suddenly turned and threw a hooking punch that glanced off his cheekbone. Surprised, Alex released her. Casey leaped away from him and began to sprint across the empty parking lot, snow flying back from her boots as she ran.

Alex had no problem catching up to her. But the way things were at the moment, Casey was bigger than he was. That made it hard for Alex to keep her under control. He leaped onto her back, knocking her facedown in the snow. Then he stood up with one arm wrapped tightly around Casey's neck.

"Come with me," he said. "Come with me, and I won't have to hurt you."

Casey relaxed for a moment, but as soon as Alex loosened his grip, she reached back, clawing for his face. He pulled her tight against him and squeezed until he heard her breath hissing out through her teeth. One of her long legs curved back, and the heel of her boot raked down Alex's shin. There was pain, but not enough to make him let go.

He lifted her from the ground and tossed her toward the car. She struck with a thud, and tried to get back to her feet. Before she could, Alex reached down and grabbed her by the back of her coat. She might be bigger, but Alex was far stronger. He lifted her easily with one hand and carried her to the car. Only when he was shutting the trunk did she think to scream. And by then it was too late.

Five inches of snow had settled on the road in front of Volker's house by the time Alex stopped and opened the front gate. It was still daylight. He glanced around, worried that he might be seen going in, but the snow was falling so fast and thick that no one could see more than a car length away. Alex pulled inside and closed the gate.

He left Casey in the car and went inside to change. He wanted to be prepared when he let her out of the trunk.

When he popped the trunk open, Casey's eyes went wide with shock. "Alex!" she cried. She sat up and looked around wildly. "I thought you were dead."

He smiled at her. "Well, I'm not dead. Come on. Let's get inside out of the cold."

She took his outstretched hand and let him help her out of the cramped trunk. "Where's Ms. Delany?" she asked as she stepped onto the snow-covered drive.

"Oh, she's around," Alex said.

Casey shook her head and brushed at the greasy dust that covered her jacket. "She's gone nuts. She . . ." Casey stopped and squinted at Alex. "How did you get here, anyway?"

He jerked his head toward the house. "Come on inside. I'll explain it to you there."

She looked up at the tall side of the house, barely visible through the driving snow. "Whose house is this?"

"Mine," Alex said.

Casey stepped back against the car. "I don't think so, Alex. I don't know what's going on here, but I think I'd rather get out of here right now." She slid along the side of the car as she talked, moving slowly away from Alex.

"I'm afraid I have to insist we go inside, Casey. Do you walk in nicely, or do I have to carry you?"

Casey launched herself away from the car, but Alex grabbed her before she could go two steps. She rained punches on him and snarled an unending stream of curses as he hauled her up the stairs into the empty house. She was still kicking and screaming when he closed the door and started up the staircase.

Alex brought her to the ruined bedroom and tossed her onto the bed. She jumped back up and started for the door, but he grabbed her again, putting one hand around her throat. He held her out at arm's length.

"Quit fighting," he said softly.

Casey's face was red and she was struggling to pull in a breath, but she screwed up her face and spat at Alex. "Let me go!" she croaked.

Alex tightened his grip until Casey's face went purple. "Quit fighting, or I'll have to really hurt you. Do you understand?"

Casey nodded.

Alex tossed her back onto the bed. "Good," he said. He bent down to the end of the bed and ripped loose a crumpled sheet. "I'm going to tie you to the bed," he said.

"Don't touch me," Casey said. Her voice was rough, and she rubbed at her bruised throat. "Stay away from me."

"I'm going to tie you down," Alex said again. "If you let me tie you down, I won't have to touch you again."

Casey made another dash for the door. Alex

caught her by the back of her coat and spun her around. He delivered a slap to the side of her head that snapped her neck back. "Stop now," he said.

For the first time, Alex saw what looked like fear in Casey's cool blue eyes. "You promise?" she said. "You promise you won't hurt me?"

"I won't have to," he said. "If you let me tie you down."

Casey leaned back on the bed. As she turned her head, she gasped. Alex followed her gaze to the jeans and sweater that were draped over the dresser. "Those were Ms. Delany's," Casey said.

Alex shrugged. "If you say so." He tore the sheet into five strips with sharp motions of his hands.

Casey cringed each time the sheet ripped. "Where is she?" she asked.

Alex moved around the side of the bed and grabbed her foot. Casey kicked out at him, but Alex caught her leg and held it. Quickly he wound a length of torn sheet around her ankle and tied it to one of the bedposts.

She turned her head to the side and looked at the rumpled clothing. "Did you do something to her?" Casey demanded. She looked down at her bound foot and swallowed. "You'd better not do anything to me, I'm warning you right now!"

Without a word Alex tied the other foot and moved to her arms. Casey flinched away, hugging herself tight. "Give me your hand,"

Alex said. "I don't want to hurt you."

"Let me go," she said. "Let me go right now, Alex, and I won't tell anyone you're here. Okay?"

He pried her arm loose and tied her wrist to the headboard. "That's good," he said. "Calm down." He walked around to the other side and took Casey's remaining wrist in his hand. "One more, and we'll be ready," he said.

Casey's eyes narrowed. "Ready for what?"

Alex pulled her hand back against the bed frame, but he didn't answer.

"Ready for what?" she repeated. She began to buck and pull at her bonds. Strong as he was, Alex had to put a knee down on her right arm to hold it still before he could manage to tie it to the bed.

Casey's back arched as she pulled at her bonds. The strips of sheet bit into her wrists and ankles as she pulled. Alex stood by until she had exhausted herself. She fell to the dirty blankets with her chest heaving in exhaustion.

"What are you going to do?" she asked weakly.

"It's an experiment," Alex said.

"Will it hurt?"

"It might," he said. "Yes, I think it probably will."

She closed her eyes. "But you said you wouldn't hurt me."

"I lied," Alex said.

Casey opened her eyes. The fear seemed to

have gone out of her. "That wasn't Ms. Delany, was it?"

"No," Alex admitted. "It wasn't."

"Are you really Alex Cole?" she asked.

Alex thought for a moment. "I'm not sure," he said. Then he took the last strip of cloth and stuffed it into her mouth.

Nineteen

Chris put down the phone. "She says she wants us over there about six thirty," he said. He turned his wrist to look at his watch. "That's only about twenty minutes from now. Is that okay with you?"

"Sure," Talli said. "It still feels kind of strange to be going over to a teacher's house for supper."

"Hey," Chris protested. "It's my house, too."

Talli grinned at him. "That makes it doubly weird," she said. "I don't think I've ever been on a date with someone when his sister was along."

"You have to give Donna a break. With my parents gone, she tries to do the job of both Mom and Dad." He stood up and joined Talli at the window. "Man, that snow's still coming down like it means to bury the town."

Talli nodded. "It was like this in November,"

she said. "I thought it would never stop snowing."

Chris looked around the room. "I like your place," he said. "I think you've got even more books than I do."

"I used to read one about every other day," Talli said. She turned away from the window and picked up a paperback from the desk. "But I guess I sort of lost interest in reading horror books after what happened with Volker." She shrugged. "Pretend monsters just didn't seem very scary or very fun anymore."

"I can understand that," Chris said.

There was a knock at the door, and Talli's father stuck his head into the room. "You sure you two don't want to stay over here for supper?" he asked. "Talli's mother won't be home till later, but I can mix up a mean bowl of chili."

Chris laughed. "Thanks, Mr. McAlister, but I think my sister has already started supper."

"Well, I guess I can let it pass this time," said Talli's father, "but I expect you to come to our house for supper real soon now. Hear me?"

"Yes, sir," Chris said. "Your father seems like a nice guy," he added after the door was closed.

"He is," Talli said. "I love my dad. Until last fall I thought there was nothing my dad couldn't do. But when Volker came for me, it was like Dad couldn't even see him. Volker did something to his mind, Chris."

Chris frowned. "If there is another one of

these things out there, I need to get a better understanding of what it can do. You said they can change shapes?"

Talli nodded. "I saw Volker turn himself into several different people."

"What about the others?" he asked. "Could they do it, too?"

"At least two of them could," Talli said. "Morris South made himself look like Lisa. He even made himself look like me. And Volker's assistant turned into some kind of werewolf."

"That's going to be a real problem," Chris said. "At least with Volker, you had a good idea of who the vampire was."

"I know," she replied. "This time it could be anyone."

There was a rattling at the window, and they both jumped. "It's only the wind," Chris said with a nervous laugh. He started to pull the paper from his pocket. He was going to ask Talli which of the missing students she *hadn't* killed, but she looked so upset that he couldn't bring himself to do it.

"Let's not worry about all this stuff right now," he said, smiling at Talli. "Let's go over and see what Donna's cooked for us and forget about vampires for tonight. We can get together tomorrow and be all responsible and worried."

Talli's smile developed slowly, but it lit up her face. "It's a deal," she said. "No worries tonight." She walked across the room and picked up her coat from the bed. "Your sister's so good at everything," she said. "I bet she's a great cook, too."

Chris laughed. "If she is, she must have just learned. The last time I remember Donna cooking anything, she was trying to make toast in a microwave."

"Then why did she invite me?" Talli asked.

"To tell the truth, I think she likes the idea of our being together."

Talli pursed her lips. "You know, I kind of like it myself," she said with a shrug. "I don't know. I was with Alex so long that it's hard to know how to feel. Somehow I feel like I'm cheating on him."

"I understand," Chris said. "Anyway, it's not like I'm asking you to marry me. Right now I'll settle for getting over there and seeing what Donna has for us to eat."

They said their good-byes to Talli's father on the way out. Opening the door at the side of the house, Chris flinched at the bite of the cold wind. "Wow. It's really getting nasty out there."

Talli leaned past him and wrinkled her nose at the sight of the blowing snow. "You think we can find your house in this?"

"I hope so," Chris said. He sank in the snow almost to his knees as he stepped away from the house. Leaning back, he offered a hand to Talli, and together they trudged down the sidewalk through the snow and the evening gloom.

At Chris's house they they began shedding their snow-crusted coats as soon as they stepped through the door. "Donna!" Chris called as he hung his damp fedora on top of his coat. "We're here."

His sister came through the door from the kitchen. She had replaced the sweater she was wearing that morning with another one in brighter colors. She smiled cheerfully when she saw them. "I'm glad you made it," she said. "I was afraid you might get lost in all this snow."

"It's bad," Chris said, "but it's not quite that bad."

"Come on into the dining room and have a seat," Donna said. "I'm going to get things ready in the kitchen."

Chris leaned over to Talli. "You must be 'company,'" he whispered. "We usually eat in the kitchen."

Talli hung her coat beside Chris's and followed him into the dining room. The table was laid out with china that Chris hadn't seen in years; in the center were a pair of tall candles.

"This is really nice," Talli said. She raised her voice and shouted toward the kitchen. "Thanks for having me over!"

"Thank you for coming," said Donna's muffled voice from the kitchen.

"Good china," Chris said in wonder. "I don't think we've ever eaten off this stuff. Donna was always afraid we might chip it." He reached down and picked up a knife from the nearest place setting. "At least she didn't get out the good silver. Then I really would be worried."

"Chris? Could you come in here and help for a minute?" Donna called.

"Sure!" Chris shouted back. He smiled at Talli. "Have a seat. Just be sure that you say good things about whatever it is she's cooking. Otherwise, I'll be hearing about it for a week."

He left Talli laughing in the dining room and pushed through the swinging door to the kitchen. Donna was leaning over the stove, stirring something that gave off clouds of steam. She looked up as he came through the door.

"Can you get something out of this cabinet for me?" she asked, pointing to the small cabinet above the stove. "It's too high for me."

"Sure," Chris said. He started across the room, but stopped when he saw a pair of men's jeans and a shirt tossed across the back of a kitchen chair. "Whose stuff is this?" he asked.

"That? I found it in the basement," Donna said. "Can you come help me?"

"Yeah, okay," Chris said, still looking at the strange clothes. He squeezed past her, and reached up to open the cabinet door. "What is it that you wanted out of here?" he asked.

"Oregano."

Chris had to stand on tiptoe to read the cans of spices that were stacked in the small space. "I don't see any. Maybe we stuck it in one of the other cabinets?" He glanced down at the pot on the stove. "You making pasta?"

Then he frowned. There were four pots on the stove, but none of them held anything but boiling water. Puzzled, he started to turn. "Donna, what are you—"

Her hand grabbed the back of Chris's hair and pulled down hard. Surprised, he lost his footing and fell back. His head struck the tile floor so hard that light flashed through his vision.

"Everything okay in there?" Talli yelled from the dining room.

Donna landed on Chris's chest, pinning both his arms under her knees and clamping one hand over his mouth. "Everything's fine," she called back to Talli. "Chris is just being clumsy."

With a smug, satisfied smile, Donna leaned down and put her face close to Chris's. "What's wrong, Chris? Afraid of your sweet sister?" Her free hand went to his throat, the smile replaced by an expression of rage.

"You had to pick Talli, didn't you, Chris?" Donna hissed. "You come into a town like this from the big city, and you think you can have any girl you want, don't you?"

Chris tried to shake his head, but the grip on his face was too tight. "I know your kind," Donna continued. "You think people in small towns are just stupid hicks. You think you can get away with anything." She shook her head. "Not this time, Chris."

The hand at his throat began to tighten. Chris kicked his heels against the floor and tried to buck her off, but she held to him like a leech. Desperately he bit at the hand over his mouth. When the fingers moved a fraction of an inch, he tried to shout, but the hand at his throat was cutting off his air, and all that came out was a painful wheeze.

The nasty smile was back on Donna's face. "Good-bye, Chris."

"Where's Donna?" he gasped.

The girl on top of him reached up and patted his cheek. "You're a smart guy, Chris. Too bad you weren't paying attention sooner." Then she reached down and worked her fingers into the front of Chris's curly blond hair. She raised his head slowly, then shoved it down hard against the floor.

A wash of shock poured over Chris, and then there was nothing but darkness.

There was another loud noise from the kitchen. "Are you sure everything's all right in there?" Talli called nervously. There was no reply, but the noises stopped. She leaned back in her chair and tried to relax. She wasn't sure she could really go along with what Chris had said and stop thinking about the other vampire. But at least for one dinner she could stop talking about it.

The doors to the kitchen opened and Talli looked up with a smile. "Do you need me to help with . . ." The words died in her mouth.

"Hello, Talli," said Alex.

"Alex," Talli whispered in shock. She stood up so quickly that her chair toppled over backward. In two steps she had her arms around him. "I thought you were dead," she said, sobbing. "Where have you been?" She ran her hands over his flannel shirt, feeling the cloth under her hand and Alex under the cloth. He was solid. He was real.

Alex smiled and ran a hand through Talli's red hair. "I got confused. When Volker had us in his office, he did something to me. It made me forget who I was for a while, but now I remember."

Talli pushed herself away from him and brushed a tear from her cheek. "Is it really you?" she asked. "Did you know your family moved out of town after you disappeared? Have you talked to your mom yet?"

"All that can wait," he said. "First I had to come back for you."

Talli looked past him at the kitchen door. "How did you know to come here? Did Chris find you, or was it Ms. Delany?" She started to push the door open, but Alex pulled her back.

"We don't need them right now," he said. "Let's go somewhere and be alone."

"But Ms. Delany . . . she was fixing something for us to eat."

Alex shook his head. "No, that was just to get you over here. She knows I was coming for you." He guided her away from the kitchen and toward the front door. "Let's go now. We've got a lot to talk about."

Talli looked back uncertainly. "But I should at least say good-bye to Chris."

"He knows what's going on, too. Come on."

Alex's grip on her arm was growing tighter as they walked. Talli's happiness began to fade. "I only want to be polite," she said.

"You can do that later," Alex said in a voice that left no room for argument.

Talli jerked her arm free. "What's wrong with you, Alex?" she snapped.

He was staring at her. His blue eyes seemed as cold as the wind howling outside. "All right. Go say good-bye to your new friends," he said.

Frowning, Talli staggered away from him. Still looking over her shoulder, she felt her way to the kitchen door. She pushed her way through and looked in, but there was no one there.

"Chris?" she called softly. "Ms. Delany, are you in here?"

On the stove something was boiling violently. Steam spit from the burners as water slopped over the sides. "Chris?" Talli called again. She walked across the kitchen and reached for the knob to turn off the burner. But she stopped short when she saw what was on the floor. She stood there with her hand stretched out over the hot stove, not even feeling the steam that was making her skin red and the sleeve of her sweater damp.

Sticking out from behind the kitchen table were a pair of legs that ended in wet sneakers. Slowly Talli turned and walked across the kitchen floor. With every step more of the body on the floor came into view. The faded jeans, the heavy flannel shirt. Then she could see the face.

There was a small pool of blood under Chris's cheek. His eyes were open, but there was nothing showing but the whites.

"You liked him, didn't you?"

Talli jumped and spun around. Alex was right behind her, his face frozen and unreadable.

"Didn't you?" he repeated.

Talli backed away, bumping into the table and sending a glass crashing to the floor. "You're like Volker," she said. "He made you a monster."

Alex held out his hand. "It's me," he said. "It's Alex. I've come back for you."

Talli shook her head sharply, her hair whipping around her face. "You're not Alex. You're just some thing that looks like Alex. Stay away from me!" Her foot bumped against Chris's leg, and his body rolled over. One arm flopped away from his chest and lay palm up on the tiles. Talli stifled a sob. "Why did you do this to Chris?"

Alex looked down at the body on the floor

with a sneer. "You couldn't wait," he said. "We were together for years, but as soon as I'm gone, you get someone else. Couldn't you have waited for me, Talli?"

Talli stepped back as Alex took a step forward. "You were dead," she said.

"I'm not dead," he said. "I'll tell you all about it, Talli. Come out of here with me and we'll talk."

"I don't want to talk. You stay away from me." Talli kept moving, sliding along with her back to the counter. She glanced to the side several times as she walked, looking for a weapon, looking for the phone, looking for anything that could help her.

Alex held out his hands. "I've worked very hard to see you tonight, Talli. You don't know how much it hurt me to come into this house. Or how much it's hurting me now to stay here. Come with me now, and I'll forgive you."

Talli reached the kitchen door and backed through it. "Forgive me?" she asked. "Forgive me for what?"

Alex pushed the door open and came after her. "I'll forgive you for forgetting about me."

She lunged for the dining-room table and snatched up a knife. "Get back," Talli said, waving the shining knife through the air. "I killed Volker, Alex. I know you can die."

He tilted his head to one side and looked at her curiously. "You killed Volker?"

"Yes. I killed Volker, and I killed all the others, too." Talli swallowed hard. "I'll kill you, Alex. If I have to. Don't make me do it."

"I wasn't sure that Volker was dead," Alex said. "Thanks for letting me know that. How did you do it? You didn't do it with a knife."

"You don't know that," Talli said. She held her knife steady. "You didn't know he was dead, so you don't know how I did it."

Alex stepped forward.

"Stay back!" Talli shouted. "I'll do it, Alex. I really will."

He stepped forward again, pushing her hand and the knife it held gently to the side. "You wouldn't kill me. I've gone through a lot for you, Talli. It's your fault that I got involved with Volker in the first place."

Talli shook her head, tears filling her eyes. "No," she whispered. "That's not true. I was trying to protect everybody."

"And look what happened." Alex brushed the tears from her eyes with the back of his hand. "Let's go, Talli."

Talli closed her eyes and slashed at him with the knife. It was not the sharpest of knives, but Talli's thrust slid into Alex's chest all the way to the handle. His blue eyes bulged, and he looked down at her in shock.

Talli let go of the knife and staggered back. "I'm sorry, Alex. I'm sorry," she whimpered.

He looked down at the knife extending from

his chest. Slowly he wrapped his fingers around the protruding handle and slid the blade free. For a few seconds a cascade of green light poured from his chest and splashed onto the floor. Then the flood slowed to a trickle. Then to nothing.

Alex dropped the knife to the dining-room floor.

"That," he said, "was a serious mistake."

Twenty

Chris moaned and rolled over. There was something wet and sticky on his face. He put a hand to the back of his head, then brought it around in front of his face. He was not surprised to see that it was covered in blood.

He got up on one elbow, but even that effort made his stomach roll. Chris rested for a moment, trying to still the storms in his head and remember what had happened. Donna had gone nuts. She had knocked him down and said something about Talli. She had . . . she hadn't been Donna.

Chris stood up fast. Black spots swam in front of his eyes, but he stayed on his feet. He turned slowly, scanning the room. Donna's clothes were on the floor near where he had been lying. The pots on the stove had boiled dry. There was a smell of burning metal in the air, and the pots pinged and rattled as they grew ever hotter.

With his eye on the door to the kitchen, Chris crossed the room and turned off the stove. He tried to be quiet as he walked to the swinging kitchen door, but his head was still swimming and he bumped against the wall several times.

There was a cardboard box sitting on the counter. Strands of shredded newspaper stuck out of the box like some kind of strange growth. Chris recognized it as the box the fake Donna must have opened to get out the good china. He reached down into the box, pushed away some paper-wrapped cups, and brought up a knife from the bottom of the box. He squeezed the handle tight as he pushed open the door to the dining room.

There was no one there. Chris stood in the doorway, swaying on his feet. He realized now that he had been far too slow. While he had been worried about ruining Talli's evening, the vampire had been plotting to take her away. Being polite had almost cost him his life and might still be the death of Talli.

He leaned against the dining table and tried to think. The vampire hadn't killed Talli, or if it had, it hadn't left her body behind. It must have taken her somewhere. From what Chris could remember of the fake Donna's words, the vampire had been very upset that Talli was going out with someone.

Chris's skull was ringing like a church bell, but he was still enough of a detective to add one and one. "Alex Cole," he said softly. It had to be. And now Alex had Talli.

The question was what he was going to do with her. Alex might have been a nice guy before, but Chris had gotten a good taste of what he was like now. And if any of the deaths in the paper were Alex's fault . . .

Thump.

Chris look up sharply, expecting to see Alex or Talli, but the room was empty.

Thump. Thump.

He looked down at the dark wood floor. The noise was coming from below. Quickly Chris dashed to the end of the hallway and flung open the door to the basement. He held the knife ready, but nothing moved in the dim shaft of light that spilled down the stairs. Then the thumping came again. It was clear that whatever was causing it was somewhere down there in the darkness.

Chris leaned into the stairway and switched on the lights. He went down into the basement one step at a time with the knife ready in his sweaty right hand. The single light bulb hung near the bottom of the steps, and it did little to clear up the inky shadows that hugged the corners of the basement. Boxes of summer clothes, paperback books, and memorabilia lay where Donna and Chris had left them a few days before. They made the basement into a kind of gloomy maze.

The thumping came again, and this time Chris could hear a muffled moan along with it.

His heart was beating as fast as a machine gun as he crept to the end of a row of boxes and peered around. He put his head against the last box and slowly leaned to the side until he could see what was making the noise.

Donna lay on the concrete floor. A piece of tan cloth was wound across her face, and her arms and legs were bound together with what looked like a twisted length of electrical cord. Her brown eyes looked up at Chris with a mixture of hope and fear.

He ran to kneel at her side. He glanced around the room. Alex didn't seem to be there at the moment. Chris dropped the knife and began to untie his sister.

"Is it really you?" she asked as soon as her mouth was clear.

"Yes," he said. "Of course it's me."

"He can look like anyone," Donna said. Her eyes swept over Chris. "But I guess you must be you. He only let me loose once, and that was only for a few minutes."

"Are you okay?"

She shook her head. "No. He did something to me. It was like he yanked all the heat out of my body. I've never felt so cold."

"I think it's Alex Cole," Chris said. "One of the students who've been missing."

Donna sat up and rubbed at her chafed wrists. "I thought it was," she said. "I saw his picture in the yearbook when I was looking up my students. But I couldn't be sure the face he was wearing was really his." Suddenly her eyes went wide. "Chris! I almost forgot about Casey."

"Casey?"

Donna nodded and climbed shakily to her feet. "I saw him bring her down the stairs a couple of hours ago. She must be down here somewhere."

It took a few minutes to find Casey lying in a dark corner, behind a row of boxes. Her blue eyes brightened as Chris came into view.

"Casey," he said with relief. "I'll have all this stuff off you in a second." Alex had tied her up far more thoroughly than he had Donna. The bonds around her arms were thick and tight. After fumbling at them for several minutes, Chris gave up in disgust. "I'll have to go get a knife for this."

Donna nodded. She was working at the strips of cloth that bound Casey's mouth. "She must have given him trouble," Donna said. "She's wrapped up like a Thanksgiving turkey."

Chris found the knife he had dropped near where Donna had been, and he ran back to Casey. The blade of the knife wasn't meant for cutting ropes, but eventually the bonds parted. At almost the same moment, Donna freed the last strap around Casey's mouth.

"You okay?" Donna asked the girl as Chris worked to free her feet.

"I'm hungry," Casey said. Her voice was dry and hoarse.

Chris laughed. "Food would be the first thing

on your mind," he said. "Don't worry. We'll get you something as soon as you're loose." He cut the first of the straps around her legs. Alex had covered the cloth with heavy fiberglass tape, and even a length of chain. Chris wondered why he had wrapped Casey so much more securely than he had Donna.

"Almost loose," Donna said. She put a hand behind Casey's head and helped the girl sit up. "Just a few seconds more."

"I'm hungry!" Casey said. This time it was almost a scream.

Chris stopped his cutting and looked at Casey. Her blue eyes were very wide, and they roamed wildly over the basement. "Something's wrong," he said.

"I think she may be in shock," Donna said. She leaned close and put her face near Casey's. "Can I get you anything?"

Casey let out a scream that rattled the window glass in its frames and raised the hairs on the back of Chris's neck. Her arms lashed up and wrapped around Donna.

Chris was frozen as he watched yellow mist stream out of Donna's eyes and mouth. Like liquid light, it cast a glow onto both his sister and Casey. With her mouth open wide, Casey greedily sucked in the energy that Donna gave off.

"No!" shouted Chris. He grabbed his sister and tried to pull her away.

Casey responded by tightening her grip. She pulled Donna so close that their faces were almost touching. Casey's eyes glowed with green light as more and more energy left Donna's body for her own.

Desperate, Chris put his fingers into Casey's brown curls and tried to pull her away from Donna. He might as well have been trying to bend a steel bar. All his strength wasn't enough to move Casey one inch.

Donna's eyes flickered and closed. The tension went out of her body, and she sagged in Casey's arms like a bag of laundry.

Everything seemed to be moving in slow motion, and yet it was all happening too fast to change. Chris scrambled across the floor and closed his hand on the knife he had been using to cut Casey free.

He lifted the blade high over his head. Casey's eyes shifted to look at him, but she didn't let go of Donna.

Chris slammed the blade down into Casey's chest.

Her arms flew open, and Donna rolled to the side. Casey's mouth gaped wide. Blue fire played over her teeth. It seemed as if flashbulbs were going off somewhere in the center of her head, showing the outline of her skull through her face. Her curly hair stood out in a cloud of brown strands, and her hands curled into claws. She beat at the blade sticking from her chest, but she couldn't seem to get ahold of it.

Chris grabbed Donna under the arms and

pulled her away from Casey. He put his hand against her throat. For the longest second of his life, he felt nothing. Then he felt her pulse under his hand. It was faint, but it was there.

Casey knocked the knife free, and it clattered across the concrete floor. Light as bright as a spotlight lanced out from the hole in her chest. She tried to cover the opening with her fingers, but it leaked past, spraying through her hands like water from a high-pressure hose.

Slowly, the jet of light grew dimmer. Its color went from white, to yellow, to a dull green glow. The emerald fire in Casey's eyes faded. As the stream of light died to a trickle, Casey rolled over and looked at Chris.

"I'm hungry," she whispered. She reached out toward him. "I'm so hungry, Chris."

He backed up, making sure he was out of her reach. "I know, Casey," he said. "I'm sorry."

She fingered the opening in her chest, looking down in wonder at the last sparks as they played around the wound. "You put a knife in me," she mumbled.

Chris nodded, tears running down his face. "I didn't want to."

She lay back on the cold floor. "I'm awfully tired," she said. "I don't think I've ever been this tired in my whole—" Her voice cut off suddenly.

Chris leaned forward. "Casey? Casey, can you hear me?"

There was a crackling sound from somewhere in Casey's chest. Her body began to shake and quiver. Veins appeared on her arms, her hands, her face. Her skin turned as gray as the basement floor. There was another noise from her chest, and a cloud of dust sprayed from the wound.

A thin wailing scream started up as Casey began to crumble. Her fingers snapped free like dead leaves falling from a tree. Then each finger crumbled into a tiny pile of gray-white powder. Her jeans and shirt shifted as the body inside fell apart. Chris had one last glimpse of her blue eyes before her skull caved in with the sound of a can being crushed. Loose teeth bounced across the floor.

Long after the last fragment of Casey had turned into dust, the screaming went on. It took Chris several minutes to realize that it was coming from him.

It was the one place Talli had never wanted to see again. As soon as she stepped through the front door of Volker's house, it was as if the last two months had never happened. The wide, empty front hall and the long curving stair to the second floor were just the same. Even the musty, abandoned smell of the place hadn't changed. She expected Volker, or his hulking assistant Lynch, to come strolling in at any second.

Alex closed the door behind her. "This is much better," he said.

"Better for who?" Talli whispered.

"We can relax here," Alex said. "We can have our talk."

Talli couldn't imagine that there was anywhere in the world where she would be less relaxed. "It's too cold in here for me," she said.

"I thought of that." Alex took her softly by the arm and steered her through a wooden door into the living room. At the far end of the room, a fire crackled in a wide stone fireplace. The room was aglow with the warm red light from the flames. There were two chairs pulled up near the fire.

Talli stood stiffly while Alex unzipped her coat and pulled it off. Then he led her over to one of the chairs. She was actually glad for the seat—her legs had felt weak ever since she realized the truth about Alex.

He sat down in the other chair and rested his hands on his knees. "It's not like you think, Talli. I'm not a monster."

"You killed Chris," she said.

Alex shook his head. "Chris isn't dead. I just knocked him out so we could have our talk."

Talli felt her heart speed up. "He's not dead?"

"No." Alex held up one hand and pointed to his eye. "I can see things now. Things that other people can't see. I can see the life in you, Talli. You're as bright as a torch to me. And I could tell that Chris wasn't really hurt." He dropped his hand and leaned back in his chair. "I don't want to hurt anyone," he said.

Talli studied Alex. In the firelight his face was warm, and his expression looked sincere. "What about Chris's sister, Ms. Delany. Where is she?"

"She's fine," he replied. "I'm really sorry that I had to tie her up and that I had to bully you. It was hurting me to be in that house, and I really wasn't thinking too well." He held up his hands and shrugged.

Alex picked up a poker from beside the fireplace and stirred the glowing cinders as he spoke. "When it first happened, it was like I couldn't think at all. I wandered all around. I can barely remember any of it. Then a few days ago I came back to Westerberg.

"It wasn't until then that I started remembering things," he continued. He reached across the gap between them and took her hands in his. "Please, Talli. I know I've done some things wrong, but this has been hard on me. I'm getting better all the time."

Confusion overwhelmed Talli. She wanted to run away from Alex. She wanted to welcome him back. How could she tell what the truth was? With all he had been through, didn't Alex deserve the benefit of the doubt? "What are you going to do now?" she asked.

"I want to be with you, Talli. That's all I've wanted since I remembered who I was." He gave her his biggest smile. "Come with me."

"Come where, Alex?" Talli asked. "Are you going to go find your parents, or go back to school?"

"I can't do those things right now," he said. "Maybe I will someday. Anyway, it doesn't matter what I do, as long as you're with me."

The chaos in Talli's mind was too much. She had to get out, had to think. "I need some time," she said. She stood up from her padded chair and brushed the hair away from her face. "I want to go home."

"Your friends will be coming after me soon," Alex said. "You've got to come with me now."

Talli walked around the chair, putting it between herself and Alex. "Come with you where, Alex? Come with you to kill people?"

"I already told you," he said. "I didn't kill anyone."

Talli had known Alex since grade school. She knew every expression of his face, and every tone of his voice. And she knew he was lying. "Give me another day," she said. "One day to talk to my parents and say good-bye to everyone."

"And then you'll come with me?"

"Yes," she said. "Then I'll come with you."

He stood up. Half his face glowed red from the firelight, the other half was invisible in the darkness. "You'll come back to me."

"Yes."

Alex shook his head. "I don't believe you. You want me to let you out of here. Then you're going right back to your new boyfriend and figure out how to kill me."

"Chris isn't my boyfriend," Talli said.

"You're coming with me now." Alex shoved the chair out of his way. His voice grew deeper. Rougher. "When you know the hunger, when you feel it burning down inside you, then you'll know that these others are nothing but food. The next time you see your Chris, you'll think of nothing but how much energy he can provide."

Talli turned and ran. She managed three steps before Alex caught her.

He was faster than she expected, and stronger than she would have believed. With one hand he trapped her arms behind her back. He ran the fingers of the other hand through her hair.

"There's something special about you, Talli," he said. His voice was soft, his lips close to her neck. "It's more than your being my girl from before. There's something special about the light in you. I think Volker saw it, too."

He turned her around to face him and tipped her chin back until she was looking into his fire-lit eyes. "When we were in his office, Volker said you would make a better vampire than me." He bent down and kissed her on the lips. "It's time to see about that." He pulled her into a tight hug.

Cold overwhelmed Talli. She felt as if she were shrinking, drawing in toward a point on a distant horizon. Her sight was gone. Her hearing and sense of touch followed. The only thing left was a sense of falling. Talli tried to fight back with arms she couldn't feel. She tried to scream, but couldn't find her mouth. There was nothing left of her.

Then Talli felt energy come into her head and surge down her spine like a bolt of ice and fire. She tried to push it back, to force it out of her body. It was like trying to put out a forest fire with a squirt gun.

As the golden fire burned all along her nerves, Talli felt more alive than she ever had in her life. Every inch of her body seemed to be humming with health. All her anxieties fell away under that blast of sheer life.

The energy was triumphant. It was the essence of youth and pleasure. She lost herself in the waves of power, finding herself drawn ever closer to the blazing furnace that was at the source of all that energy. She reached the blinding heart of power.

Eagerly, she rushed out to greet it, to merge with it, to bathe in its wonderful glow.

Twenty-one

Chris beat at the gate. Each blow of his hammer rang out like the sounding of an iron bell, but the waves of snow swallowed up the sound. It took ten blows to bash apart the heavy chain that had been wrapped around the damaged lock. His frostbitten fingers pressed against the bars, and the gate swung inward with a squeal.

He slogged up the snow-choked driveway to the front door of the house. The wind had erased any sign that someone else might have come this way. Chris mounted the steps to the front porch and peered into the glass at the side of the door. There was no one in sight. He tried the doorknob and found it locked. He held up the hammer and weighed it in his hand. If he smashed open the door and it was the wrong house, he could get into big trouble. If he didn't smash open the door and it was the right house . . .

He smashed open the door.

As soon as he was inside, Chris knew he had made the right decision. There was an electric hum pulsing through the house. It sounded like a generator run mad. He reached into his coat pocket, took out his knife, and started across the room. At first he thought the noise was coming from above, but two steps up the staircase, he realized it was coming from behind the paneled door to his right.

His boots left puddles of melting snow on the bare wood floor as he crossed to the door. He pushed on the door harder and harder, and was about to resort to his hammer, when he realized that the door swung the other way. Gently, he tugged on the knob.

The scene behind the door was like something from a nightmare. Flames that boiled in the fireplace at the end of the long room gave everything a hellish red color. There was a mingled smell of burning wood and ozone. It smelled very much like a tree that had been hit by lightning.

In the center of the room Talli and Alex stood wrapped in each other's arms. Bolts of green and blue lightning swarmed over them like writhing snakes. Alex's eyes were open, and he looked down at Talli with an expression of expectant glee. More terrible than that was Talli's face. Her eyes were closed, and her head was tilted back. She seemed to be experiencing something close to pure joy.

Alex's head turned slowly, and his eyes fixed on Chris. "Stay back," he said. Ribbons of fire rolled out of his mouth as he spoke. "It's too late to help her now."

Talli moaned out in pleasure and moved her hands up Alex's back. A wide smile split Alex's face, and blue sparks chased themselves along his teeth. "You better get out of here now, Chris. When we get done with this, my girlfriend here is going to be very, very hungry."

Chris snarled and dashed forward. Alex's hand snapped out like a striking cobra. The force of the blow was enough to send Chris spinning across the room. He steadied himself and came forward more slowly, the knife poised in his hand.

Alex opened his mouth and laughed. "Better put that knife away before you hurt yourself with it," he said. "Knives don't work on me."

"We'll see about that," Chris said. He slashed out with the blade.

Talli wondered why she had ever worried about going with Alex. Everything was light. Each time she thought she had reached the peak of the power, she found another, brighter source lying ahead. She flashed through each barrier, reveling in what she found there. Moving ever faster, she plunged into the brightest, warmest core of energy yet—and found it full of blackness.

The faintest fear began to taint the happiness she had been feeling. How could this slick darkness lie at the heart of so much warmth and life? She reached out to it. The darkness was not empty. Something lived in it. It brushed against Talli. She felt only the barest touch of it, but she knew what it was. A bottomless void that hungered for life. A gulf that could never be filled.

She tried to pull away from it. She wanted to go back and up, back into the warmth where she felt safe and strong. But the blackness followed her. With every touch she could feel it carving out a place in her soul. Like a swimmer in deep water, she no longer knew which way was up. Darkness hung in every direction, and in Talli's heart, the hunger grew.

Then she was staggering away, her eyes blind and her stomach rolling. She fell to a hard floor and lay there with a cold wind blowing over her face.

There was a bellow of rage, and Talli opened her eyes to see Alex staring down at a knife that jutted from his side. She looked around the room for Chris and finally found him on the floor at the base of the far wall. He was on his knees, one hand over his face. Blood dripped through his fingers.

"I told you a knife wouldn't stop me!" shouted Alex. He reached down and grabbed the knife by the handle. Then he hissed and pulled back his hand. "What is this?" he asked. He grabbed for the knife again. Again he jerked back as he touched the bare metal. Finally, growling in frustration, he reached down and seized the knife.

Smoke rose from his hand as he pulled at the blade, but Alex held on and jerked the knife free. He dropped it to the floor and scowled down at his scorched hand.

He advanced on Chris with the speed of a striking snake. Seizing him by the sweater, Alex lifted him up until Chris's feet dangled several inches above the floor. As Chris's hands beat at Alex's arm, Talli could see the cut that ran down his cheek. She had no doubt that Alex had put it there.

"Now you'll have to pay for hurting me," Alex snarled.

"Alex, no!" Talli screamed. She was so dizzy that the floor seemed to pitch like the deck of a ship in a hurricane, but she climbed to her feet and staggered toward him. "Please let him go."

Alex's face tightened into a mask of rage. "No. If I don't get rid of him, you'll never love . . . never . . ." He blinked, and his expression changed to surprise. He looked down at his side.

Light was beginning to dribble out. At first it was as thick and slow as the blood that leaked from the cut on Chris's face. Then the flow sped up.

Alex tossed Chris aside. "I can heal this," he

said. "I've taken much worse." His eyebrows knit together in concentration. The flow of liquid light grew even faster. It splashed at his feet and made an electric green puddle on the floor. Alex grunted with effort, but the hole in his side only widened. He glared at Chris.

"What did you do to me?" he demanded. "What was that knife?"

Chris smiled. "The good silver," he said.

Alex tried to staunch the flow of energy with his hand, but with no more luck than Casey had had. As the flow through his fingers grew into a flood, he turned to Talli with horrible pain twisting his face. "I need more energy," he said. "Give me some of yours. Just a little, Talli."

Talli remembered the blackness that lay at the core of Alex's power. "No," she said. "I can't." There was no such thing as "just a little" to that aching emptiness.

"You have to," Alex said. "I *need* it, Talli."

Chris dashed past him and snatched up the knife from the floor. "Stay away from her," he said firmly. "Stay back, Alex, or I'll give you another cut."

Alex hissed, but he backed up. He walked across the room slowly, each footstep seeming to require an enormous effort, and collapsed into one of the chairs. A trail of light marked his passage across the floor.

The flow of energy from his side was slowing, but Talli didn't think the wound was healing.

Alex's face was becoming drawn and thin. "I can heal this," he said again, but his voice was hollow and strained. He slumped in his chair, his chin hanging down against his chest.

Chris came over to Talli and put an arm around her shoulders. "Are you okay?" he asked.

Talli nodded. "I think so. One more minute, and I might not have been able to say that."

Alex looked up. There was an audible groan as he moved his neck. Talli had to put a hand over her mouth to keep from crying out when she saw his face.

Alex was little more than a skeleton. His lips peeled back to show the base of yellowing teeth. His nose was nothing but a hole in his face. His blue eyes rolled in sockets ringed with empty space. "I just wanted you back," he said.

"Alex," Talli said. "I'm so sorry."

His head fell back against his chest. The flow of light from his side had ceased.

"Alex," Talli said softly. Her chest felt tight, and air burned as she pulled it through her aching throat.

"It's all over now," Chris said. "Finally over."

Talli nodded, her eyes still on the slumped form in the chair. "At least now I know what happened to him," she said. She swallowed and cleared her throat. "Is your sister really all right?" she asked.

"She's weak," Chris said. "Alex did something to her, but I think she'll recover." He took her by both hands. "Talli, Casey's dead."

"Casey? How?"

"Alex did to her what he wanted to do to you," he said. "He made her into a thing that lived on energy stolen from other people."

Talli couldn't think of anything to say. Of everyone at school, no one seemed more alive than Casey. It was impossible to think she was gone.

"Come on," Chris said. "Let's get out of this place." He helped Talli toward the front hall.

"Wait," she said. "I need my coat." She pointed to where Alex had left her coat near the fire, and Chris hurried across the floor to get it.

Chris turned back with a grim smile on his face. "We'll go back over to my house and check on Donna," he said. "Then I'll get you home."

Talli nodded. "Fine."

Suddenly Chris stopped in midstride. His eyes rolled back and he toppled to the floor.

A terrible form stood behind him. Nothing more than bones covered in a dry parchment skin, Alex leaned over the fallen body. His joints squealed and squeaked with every movement.

The bony head turned to Talli. "I told you I could heal it," he said in a voice as dry as dust. "I'll take his energy, and then we'll leave."

He turned his ruined face to Chris and opened his mouth. Tendrils of smoky light began to drift up from all over Chris's body.

They turned into a twisting rope of fire that poured into Alex's gaping mouth.

Talli ran forward and kicked at Alex. The noise her boot made on his ribs was like an ax striking wood. Alex fell off Chris and rolled to the edge of the fireplace. One of his arms fell into the fire, and flames leaped up his sleeve.

Talli saw that it wasn't only the cloth that was burning. Alex's hand itself was on fire. She grabbed Chris by one arm and started dragging him across the floor.

Alex crawled after her. The flames spread across his back and down his other arm. His brown hair went up in a sudden blaze, leaving nothing on his head but a cap of black stubble.

Talli pulled as hard as she could, but Alex was catching up. With each agonized movement of his arms, he drew closer. The fire was all over him now. A flaming scarecrow, he looked up at Talli with a face scorched free of all flesh.

Bony fingers closed on Chris's ankle. Talli screamed and tugged backward as hard as she could.

Alex's arm broke in two at the elbow. Like a table that had lost one leg, he fell to his side. The bare, blackened jawbone moved one last time, and Talli was terrified that he might still say something. All movement stopped. There was nothing left on the floor except a burning pile of bones and cloth.

Talli kept pulling, dragging Chris backward.

She stopped at the doorway and looked back.

Fire had begun to move out from Alex's body. It was scorching the wooden floor and licking up the legs of one of the chairs. It would have been easy to put out the fire. Talli could have done it in a few minutes.

She let it burn.

Chris didn't wake up until she had pulled him outside into the snow. The storm had blown over, and a million stars glittered in the velvet black sky.

They sat on the porch for several minutes. The smell of smoke from inside grew stronger, and at last they stood up and pushed their way home through the snow.

Epilogue

Talli woke up and rolled over in her bed. It had been late when she left Chris's house, and after that the sound of fire engines had kept her up well past midnight. She was surprised to see that she had woken up while it was still dark outside.

She stood up and glanced out the window. The sky in the east was scarlet with the coming day. Where the tall sides of Volker's house had been, there was nothing but a few streamers of watery white smoke drifting into the winter air. Talli yawned and stretched her arms out over her head; then she walked across the room and leaned against the window frame.

Alex was gone, but Alex had really been gone since November. As Chris had said, it was finally over. And this time Talli had a feeling that he was right. The cloud that had hung over

Westerberg since Volker first came into town had finally lifted.

The sun peeked over the horizon, and orange light filled the tops of the bare winter trees. The blanket of snow on the ground outside caught the light, and for a moment the whole world seemed made out of gold.

Talli smiled. It seemed that everything was suddenly as it should be.

Sunlight streamed through her window, gleaming off the snow on the ledge outside. Talli screamed and stepped back.

Everywhere the sunlight touched her, her skin was black and smoking.